PEBBLES ON THE STRAND

AN ANTHOLOGY OF CONTEMPORARY SHORT STORIES

edited by Ian Gouge

Coverstory
books

First published in by Coverstory books, 2024

Paperback ISBN 978-1-7393569-4-1
ebook 978-1-7384693-0-7

www.coverstorybooks.com

PEBBLES ON THE STRAND

AN ANTHOLOGY OF CONTEMPORARY SHORT STORIES

Contents

✿

Over the Edge and into the Wind

The heels of his brown boots dug into the rocky edge of the bluff, the scuffed tips pointing out over the rim and into the cool open air. Michael tilted his body toward the wind and the vast empty space before him, arms stretching out from his shoulders like Jesus on the Cross. Tony's right hand clutched the tail of Michael's denim shirt, his left arm hooked around the branch of a juniper tree. The only thing between the end of Michael's nose and the dry creek bed below were 300 feet of mountain air.

"Isn't that freakin' amazing?" Tony said, laughing. "Feel it, man? Feel all of it? It's as free as you'll ever get. Ever!"

Michael closed his eyes and leaned all his weight into the abyss, flapping his one free arm as if he were about to take flight. "My ... GOD! This, this is ... unbelievable!" Tony snatched Michael from the cliff's edge, and they wrapped their arms around each other in celebration of shared adrenaline.

"Holy shit!" Michael hollered into the canyon. The two of them jumped in the air, slapping each other on their backs.

Tony rushed to the edge. "Do it for me," he said, pulling his tee shirt over his head and throwing it to the ground. "Grab my belt loop."

"You serious?" Michael asked, questioning Tony's trust.

"Put your fingers through it and hang on, man." Tony inched the toes of his shoes just over the edge of the bluff and bent into a crouch. Michael stuck the index and middle fingers of his right hand into the belt loop of Tony's jeans. Tony stood, reached his hands around his head, and clasped them behind his neck the way criminals do on those TV cop shows, and shifted his weight into the broad chasm.

"This is what life should always feel like! I never, EVER want to die!" Tony howled.

It was earlier that morning when the shadows were long that Tony saw Michael hitchhiking along the highway outside Santa Fe and offered him a ride.

Michael leaned into the open window on the passenger side of Tony's car, an old Mazda, the color faded by the sun. "Where you headed?" he asked.

"You know, man," Tony said, smiling. "I'm not really sure." He tapped the steering wheel with the palm of his right hand and then his left, as if striking a snare drum and its rim. "But I'm pointed west and if that's where you're pointed, we can keep each other company."

Michael grabbed his canvas backpack from the gravel of the road's shoulder, threw it into the car's back seat, and jumped into the front. He had spent the night sleeping on a bench outside the Deming Airport. He had been out for a couple of hours on a stretch of Route 549, starting at just before dawn, walking and thumbing. It seemed like hundreds of cars and trucks had whizzed by him, throwing exhaust and dust into his face. Someone in a U-Haul truck slowed down and pulled over, but as Michael ran to the door, the driver hit the gas and sped off. It was just a few minutes later that someone else in a convertible, some expensive car, an Audi he thought, gave him the finger as he zipped by yelling, "Get a job!" With five days of stubble, his hair pulled back in an uneven ponytail, and a day-old wash-up in the dirty restroom of an old Shell gas station somewhere between Albuquerque and Santa Fe, Michael didn't look much like a man after a job.

Michael wrote poetry. He returned to New Mexico two years earlier, hoping to find a reason to keep writing. He spent a few years in St. Louis in a third-floor studio apartment with two old friends from college. One was a painter, the other a dancer. Michael worked part time at a tiny independent bookstore. His roommates also had part time jobs. One was an attendant at a small fitness center in Uptown, cleaning locker rooms and wiping away the sweat left behind on treadmills and elliptical machines. The other was a cashier at an adult video store on a highway just outside town. Michael knew he needed a change when his roomies started buying more dope than food. But he knew it wasn't just a matter of roommates and apartments. His reasons for leaving were bigger. Michael's father still lived in New Mexico, outside Las Cruces, and although his friends believed he was returning to be around family, Michael knew that was far from the truth. Any interest Michael may have had for reconnecting with his father had faded like his friends' dreams. Michael was hoping New Mexico might give him emotional familiarity, a good place for a fresh beginning, a place to jump-start his writing, bring back old memories from a childhood when his mother was alive, and his father was interested. Maybe the desert would remove him from other temptations, help him find his voice. During his time in St. Louis, he had one poem printed in a college poetry journal and another in a former student's online start-up literary site, but mostly it had been a time of unanswered submissions and uninspired writing.

Michael found work as a substitute teacher in Las Cruces and rented a one-room apartment not far from New Mexico State.

Even though it was hard not to consider it, he never tried to contact his father. Michael's mother died when he was just starting college, and after that his dad vowed to never leave the home that they'd shared throughout their 20-year marriage, digging his heels into a life of sullenness, unemployment checks, food stamps, and distancing himself from his son. Michael could understand his father's sadness, but not his rejection. Michael telephoned, emailed, and wrote letters to his father nearly every week during his first year in St. Louis, then every month, and then he stopped, giving up when there was never a response. The letters came back unopened.

Summer came and the part time teaching job ended. Michael put two tee-shirts, his journals, and a book of Ginsberg poems in a duffle bag and stood along Route 478, hoping to eventually head west. He didn't know exactly where he was going, but that was the idea. During the school year, Michael wrote in fits and starts, deleting words, lines, and sometimes complete poems from his computer. What he thought New Mexico might offer it hadn't. It was time to try something different, yet again. Michael now believed he needed to just move, travel, see, and feel new things, abandon recognizable surroundings. Maybe somewhere out there was that one thing in another place and time, a spontaneous experience that would help him finally create what he still believed he could.

It was just west of Deming on Route 418 that Tony stopped to let Michael in his car.

"What's your story, man?" Tony asked. He flicked his steel Zippo lighter, the small flame igniting his Winston, producing a red glow at the cigarette's end. The window on the driver's side was rolled down a quarter to allow the ashes to disappear into the rushing wind.

"No story," Michael said. "Just trying to get out of my own way."

Tony took a drag of his cigarette, bluish smoke rushing out his nostrils. "Come on, everyone has a story, my friend."

Tony was five years older than Michael and dressed as if he had spent a considerable amount of time listening to R.E.M, the independent rock band from the 1990s — gray t-shirt, black jeans, a thick pewter ring on the middle finger of his left hand, a mix of hipster and hippie. He even looked a bit like R.E.M.'s lead singer, Michael Stipe — thin build, almost gaunt, a shaven head showing the faint outline of male-pattern baldness, two-day growth of beard.

"My story, huh?" Michael asked, scratching his own whiskers. "Do you know much about poetry?"

"What is it you want to talk about, man? Rilke? Rimbaud? Dylan? Cobain?"

"Sounds like you have some definite thoughts."

"I read a bit. Listen to great songwriters."

"Have a favorite?"

"That's always tough. Depends on my mood."

"Pick one."

Tony blew smoke out of the side of his mouth and then looked Michael up and down. "You," he said.

"Me?"

"Yeah, you're a poet, aren't you?"

Michael smiled and turned to look out the passenger side window. "How the hell did you know that?"

"I could tell. And today, you are my favorite."

For several hours along I-10 through Lordsburg, San Simon, Bowie, Wilcox, and Tucson, Michael and Tony talked about poets, writing, songs, girls, school, and work. Michael told him a little about growing up in New Mexico, but never mentioned his father. He talked about St. Louis, his stoner roommates, and his love of good words and his struggle to write them. "Oh, I know about loving something so much, about having a passion," Tony said. "And I know what it feels like when you can't satisfy it, and something, whatever it is, gets in the way." Tony had played guitar in a rock band in Atlanta, but the band broke up when the lead singer settled down to start a family. Tony took a job managing a crew of landscapers outside Birmingham, Alabama, just to get some cash. His silly attempt to forget about music failed and breaking his back hauling dirt and digging tree holes for rich people with big lawns quickly got old. "Worked for about a month. And my Spanish sucked. I couldn't talk to the workers," he said. So, Tony took all the money he had out of his bank account — about $5000 — and started driving. "Through Arkansas and Texas and then to New Mexico." Tony grew up in Cleveland. "The home of Rock-n-Roll," he said proudly. "But I hate that town."

Outside Tucson, Tony and Michael bought pre-wrapped turkey sandwiches and several bottles of Miller beer at a 7-Eleven, topped off the gas tank, and hopped back on I-10 westbound to Phoenix.

"I'm thinking San Francisco," Tony said, unwrapping a new pack of cigarettes. "What do you say, man?"

The ride had turned out to be a good one. Michael liked Tony. And even though he was hoping for some quiet time somewhere along the road so he might try writing, Michael was enjoying himself. Something he wasn't exactly used to doing.

"Good plan," Michael said. "I've never been there."

"But first, before the city, I need some off-road stuff. I want badlands or something," said Tony. He pulled the car onto the shoulder and opened the map that had been crudely folded and tucked between the front seats. "Let's go here," he said, his index finger tapping the map and pointing to the Prescott National Forest."

Michael smiled. "Rock-n-Roll. Let's do it."

Tony swiftly turned the car from the shoulder and onto the concrete, tires squealing as he zoomed into the left lane of the highway. The Allman Brother's "One Way Out" blared from the radio's speakers, some classic rock radio station he tuned into as he drove out of Phoenix, and simultaneously Tony and Michael rolled down their windows and moaned the bluesy lyrics into the wind, "There's a man down there, might be your man, I don't know!"

Driving north on I-17, Tony and Michael drank their bottles of beer and tried to guess the songs on the radio. Whoever recognized the song first and could yell out the name was entitled to a swig of the other's beer. Tony was good with songs before 1980, but Michael was a killer with anything after 1990. The decade of the 80s was a toss-up, considering Michael was born in 1985 and Tony was just a kid.

"I remember my dad had a David Bowie album," Michael said. It was the first time he had mentioned his father during the ride. "That was the 80s, right?"

"I think." Tony shrugged. "Wasn't Journey big then too? Hate that group."

"My father had a Journey record, too, I'm sure," said Michael.

Tony sang out the opening lines to the chorus, the signature lyric from the most famous of Journey's hit records. "But, you know, I like your old man better for his love of Ziggy Stardust."

Michael leaned back in his seat and tossed back what was left of the final bottle of beer. "Yeah, I heard a lot of that record," he said, closing his eyes.

"Rolling Stones," Tony said, nodding at the radio. "I'm thinking, what, 1970?"

"You got me," said Michael, his eyes still closed. "And I'm out of beer, anyway."

Tony laughed. "I win, but I lose, right?" He turned off the radio. "Bet Dad had some Stones albums."

"Probably," Michael said, adjusting his seat so he could lean back even farther.

"I don't remember what albums my father had around the house," said Tony. "Didn't pay attention, I guess. Didn't pay much attention to anything he did. Tried not to."

There were beats of silence and then Michael asked, "Ever see him?" He opened his eyes and turned his head toward Tony. "Ever talk to him?"

"Not in years."

"He alive?"

"Haven't heard otherwise. Spoke with my brother about a year ago. Never mentioned him."

"Didn't get along, huh?"

"Not sure I ever knew him." Tony reached again for the Winston pack on the dashboard. "Not sure he really wanted me to."

"Haven't talked to my dad in a long time," said Michael. "He just kind of gave up on me. It was after Mom died. Not sure I completely understand it. I guess I gave up on him." Michael turned on the radio again. "R.E.M.," he said, confidently. "Losing My Religion."

"Shit, man," laughed Tony. "You didn't even give me a chance."

Michael put a fist close to his mouth, pretending to hold a microphone and belted out the lyrics to the chorus. Tony joined in.

The remainder of the ride north was filled with songs from the radio and dozens of guesses — Neil Young, Metallica, Green Day, John Hiatt, Sublime. But Tony and Michael were no longer keeping count, and with the empty bottles tossed on the backseat floor, there was no longer the reward of a mouthful from the other's beer. The songs that had once been the answers in a simple trivia game, were now markers in the musical score of two lives, the soundtrack for what they hoped to always remember and some of what they wanted to forget.

Prospectors once panned for gold in Lynx Creek in the Prescott National Forest, adventurers searching for precious stones that would transform their lives, settle their debts, or offer them new and better choices. Today you can still hunt for gold along the creek bed, even where it had dried into hard ground. But when Michael and Tony entered Prescott, they knew nothing of past or present riches in and around the valley. Instead, they walked to the first trailhead they saw, a slow climbing hike through scrub and pinyon pine and then to higher elevations of rocky hills and juniper.

"Can you imagine the stars out here?" Tony asked.

"I've slept in the desert before," said Michael, "and the stars are incredible, but it's the sounds of the night you remember. Beautiful and spooky."

"Scorpions crawling in the sleeping bag?" Tony asked, smiling.

"Never had one in the bag, but you just know they're around."

For the next half-hour, Michael and Tony said little, allowing space in time for their eyes to survey the desert and their minds to imagine life out here in the wide-open world, away from the towns and cities, away from everything. It would be peaceful, they both believed, void of outsiders and influences. It would be a natural life, an authentic life, harsh but real. It was Thoreau who asked men to live deliberately, but Michael knew he lacked the courage to live anything like the man of Walden and found his philosophy, his way of living, to be unrealistic, nearly impossible in a modern life. Still, wild and wide-open spaces had always given Michael new confidence in the world. Like Thoreau, Michael knew nature fed his soul.

It's partly why he returned to New Mexico. Maybe, he thought, men could live thoughtfully, with intent, if they let the natural world guide them, even if only in a small way. Many times, when Michael found himself along the secluded stretches of Chicago's lakefront, or under trees in one of the city's big parks, or near an arroyo in New Mexico where he had grown up and to where he had returned, he would consider what it would be like to commit to such a life.

"What a view," Tony called out to Michael who had fallen a bit behind on the trail. "This is what it's all about, man."

Deep greens of pines and browns of desert rock contrasted with the blue sky that touched the tops of the distant mountains.

"Makes you want to fly right out into all of it," Michael said as he stepped to the rocky cliff beside Tony.

Tony smiled, "And that's what we're going to do, my friend. I'm going to help you fly."

The next day, Michael and Tony traveled 500 miles to San Francisco, drove across the Golden Gate, walked through the Haight, downed late-night beers in North Beach, then found a room at the Crystal Hotel — what some called a flophouse on Eddy Street — to sleep away the long ride from Arizona, each taking turns on the floor and the bed. In the morning on the wooden table near the door, Michael found a napkin slid under a hard plastic bathroom cup, a crushed cigarette butt still smoking. On the napkin was a handwritten note.

I hope you find what you want, and always write what you love.

Tony.

Michael sat on the floor and cried.

That fall, Michael found himself back in Las Cruces. He had taken a full-time job teaching English at the high school, and in the early mornings he had made it his routine to steep a pot of tea, sit at his small kitchen table and look out the window toward the Organ Mountain range, and write verse that mattered to him. And sometimes on the weekends, Michael would roll out his sleeping bag on the stony desert ground to sleep under the Southwestern stars and dream of flying above it all.

David W. Berner

Hard Cheese

I had no earthly way of amusing myself once I got arrested and locked up at Juvenile Hall. The boredom was a dull, never-ending thud in my head, a silent continuous pin prick to each of my arms and legs. There was no girls' basketball team, no rock polishing, no photography, no classes like the ones Nan signed me up for at the neighborhood Y. And I had only two words for the food I ate so that I wouldn't pass out from starvation: "hard cheese", an expression I learned from a book of old phrases and which could be used to describe every kind of bad situation. There were no hot dogs on a stick, no barbecued beef on a bun, no burgers, and no spicey Cheetos. This was how it felt to be in custody when I just turned fourteen years old.

I did not have any friends at Juvie. The other girls who were there wondered whether I was a white girl or a black girl. When they asked me what I was, I would tell them I was off-white. The truth is that I was not actually sure of my skin color. I did not look like my white mother, and I never knew my father, who, as far as I could tell, was just another one of my mother's many boyfriends who came and went.

It took no time for me to realize that there was nothing to do at Juvenile Hall but read. I read big books and studied big words. I looked up the meaning of words in an old Webster's dog-eared, paperback dictionary that I found on the floor of the girl's bathroom. I collected words the way I used to collect smooth pieces of glass at Point Lobos beach with my mother. I would troll the library for different books, and I discovered all sorts of new words every day. I imagined putting those words in my mouth, turning them over with my tongue, then spitting them out in anger at the social workers who came to see me. Sometimes I would spit out these new words at my public defender who asked me too many questions. I believed I was slowly going mad with *taedium vitae*, which had become my newest of all new phrases. I demanded to be taken out of mandatory summer school to see the nurse so I could tell her I was suffering from *taedium vitae*. She looked this phrase up on her iPad and sent me back to class.

It didn't matter that I refused to study or that I never tried to learn anything taught in the summer school we were forced to attend. All the students at Juvenile Hall received either As or Bs on their report cards. I believed that the teachers felt sorry for us and thought that giving us good grades would help build our self-esteem. They thought that all of us had low self-esteem because of our rotten lives. I think I esteemed myself quite highly in those days, but I knew that the teachers felt even more sorry for kids like me who had no aunts or uncles or mothers or fathers to come visit them on visiting day. Once in a while a few kids actually did have both a mother and a father pay them a visit. I had only my grandmother, Nan, who was too old and too crippled to take the M streetcar all the way down to Juvenile Hall. Back then my mother was locked up in her own kind of sorrowful *taedium vitae*. Her life had always been hard cheese.

Before I was locked up, I spent much of my time after school by myself in front of our apartment collecting rocks or walking over to Mr. Tang's Liquors to buy myself a Coke. The gardens of the neighboring houses were made up of blown-out tires, worn-out refrigerators, and rusted car parts on gravel. Sometimes I would find interesting rocks in the gravel of those yards. Mr. Richardson would sit on the front porch of his broken-down house next door and stare at me as I bent over to collect my specimens. He never moved from his wicker peacock chair, which at first made me wonder whether or not he had any legs at all underneath the blanket that was piled on top of his lap. His face was young, but he acted old by sitting outside his house every day, doing nothing at all. He never said hi, he never waived, and he never asked about my mother, but I knew he was watching me. It was this act of watching that eventually ended up saving my life and putting my mother in rehab just five weeks before my own arrest. While I was at Juvenile Hall I thought more about my mother and the part I played in her being taken away than I did about my own confinement. I stayed up late at night agonizing about why I let the paramedics into our apartment. I hated myself for letting them in.

The day my mother was put into rehab I had gone to Mr. Tang's with a handful of change I had taken out of the spare-change purse on our kitchen counter. I had enough money to buy a coke and three pieces of *muy*, which was a kind of sweet and sour Chinese plum candy wrapped in cellophane that Mr. Tang kept in a jar on a top shelf behind the counter. I also took a free butterscotch sucking candy from a small dish by the register where it sat alongside the pennies Mr. Tang left out for everyone to use.

After I walked back to our apartment building, I remember setting down the coke, opening the wrapper on the butterscotch candy and popping it into my mouth. The candy was large, my mouth was small, and I accidentally sucked it in such a way that the butterscotch immediately became lodged in the back of my throat. I tried to dislodge it with my tongue, then with my fingers by shoving my pointer fingers into the back of my throat, but I could not pry the candy loose. I began gasping for air and struggling to breathe. Mr. Richardson, always watching, must have seen what was happening from his front porch, so he got off his peacock chair and rushed down his steps to help me. He started pounding on my back, but I kept making loud heaving noises and continued to gag and choke. When he saw that the pounding on my back was not effective, he grabbed me underneath my arms, lifted my slight body upside down and began shaking me and dangling me by my ankles. I continued to struggle to breathe, and suddenly the tuna fish sandwich and glass of milk I ate for lunch earlier that day came rushing up from my stomach and out of my mouth, half digested. He was strong enough to continue holding me upside down by my ankles. The more he shook me the more liquid and half-digested food particles would leave my stomach and splatter out of my mouth onto the pavement. I thought I was going to die until the large piece of candy finally dislodged itself from my throat and tumbled onto the sidewalk.

He sat me down on the sidewalk and then sat down next to me until both of us were able to catch our breaths. Then he left me alone, walked inside his house, and called 911. The paramedics arrived in an ambulance almost immediately while I was still sitting wiping throw up from my hair with my hands. Mr. Richardson told them in low whispers what had happened and pointed out the building where I lived. One of the female paramedics listened to my chest with a stethoscope, asking me to breath in and out five times. She then asked to speak with my mother. She smiled at me in such a kind way, and given all the excitement I did not think to tell her that my mother was not at home. I took her and two other paramedics up to our apartment, hoping that my mother would be awake and dressed. When I pushed open the unlocked door where we lived, they saw my mother lying in a semi-conscious state on the sofa next to a mostly empty bottle of gin. They looked around and also saw that we had left trash and moldy food lying around. I tried to explain that we cleaned up on Fridays and since it was only Wednesday our apartment was not ready to be cleaned. At that point they were no longer focused on me or on my ability to breathe. They were focused only on my mother.

Phone calls were made to child protective services, two paramedics carried my mother out the door on a stretcher and into the ambulance, while the third waited with me until the child protective worker finally came and took me to an emergency shelter for the night. I was given the lower bunk bed in a room with three other girls, but before I had time to settle in, that same worker took me into a small interview room without windows. Each wall of the room was painted with gray elephants and floating yellow balloons near the ceiling. I noticed that one of the elephants was brown-stained and peeling from an old ceiling leak. The protective services worker began asking me more questions and made me repeat the whole story about the butterscotch sucking candy and my mother's sleeping habits. She asked about the rooms filled with garbage and I again tried to tell her that Friday was our cleanup day, but she did not seem interested in anything I had to say on this subject. She wanted to know if my mother's boyfriends ever hit me. I was overjoyed when Nan finally came to pick me up the next morning.

Hugging Nan was like hugging a large double-wide feather pillow. She lived only five blocks away from our apartment, but I seldom saw her because she did not get along with my mother. Her street seemed like it was in a different country all together compared to where I lived. There were young men hanging out on street corners speaking Spanish and girls who were just a little bit older than me sitting on the steps of apartment buildings smoking cigarettes. There was a Korean grocery down the street and a taco truck right around the corner from Nan's house. Nan said that I could keep going to my same school in the fall. She gave me a bedroom to sleep in, and her house smelled nice like fabric softener.

Only a week after I came to live with Nan, I was approached by a girl who often sat across from Nan's house on the fire escape of her building to watch people who were out on the street. She told me her name was Monica, that she was sixteen and a half, and that she was the head of a girl's gang called the She-Dogs. She said that only girls could be members, and that there were girls on Nan's block who belonged. She proudly let me know that she had recently been arrested for selling drugs at school. She said that the cops tried to get her to snitch on her supplier, but that she would sooner be caught dead than ever be a snitch. Snitches got beaten up. I told her that her gang sounded like a girl's club I once belonged to and asked about the types of activities this club liked to do. She smiled and said that, maybe if I was lucky enough to become a member, I would find out.

I stopped collecting rocks from gravel yards and began to hang out with Monica and the She-Dogs when school ended for the summer. Nan wanted me to stay away from them, which is why she signed me up for the summer classes at the Y. She called the girls "iron-clad troublemakers," and said they reminded her of my mother. I refused to listen because these girls were nice to me and treated me like I belonged, even though I was at least two years younger than most of them. I helped them pick out their tight jeans and paint-splashed tee shirts, I admired their eye shadows and lip glosses, and I danced with them to their favorite metal and rock bands. I listened intently when they talked about all of the bad boys who were in a street gang all their own, and who liked breaking into locked cars.

It took no time at all for Monica to tell me that I was going to be initiated into her gang. She said that I would soon be the youngest member and went on to instruct me to follow her and to do everything she and the other girls did that day. I followed the She-Dogs all afternoon. Around 4:00 we walked five blocks back to the area where my mother and I had lived before she was taken away. I tried to swing my hips the way the other girls did as we walked, which made them laugh, and I told them stories about people who used to live on my block. Eventually we ended walking by Mr. Tang's Liquors. Monica told me to watch her closely and do everything that she and the other girls did once they entered the store. When we walked inside, I said hi to Mr. Tang as Monica and the three other girls took bottles of wine off the shelf and tucked them under their arms. I knew they were underage and could not buy alcohol, but figured that they probably had fake I.D.'s. I watched them each walk past Mr. Tang without stopping at the cash register to pay. I stood still and continued to watch them, but I did not follow them. Mr. Tang stopped Monica by putting his hand on her shoulder as the other girls ran quickly out of the store. Monica held the bottle of wine under her left arm, lifted her shirt with her right arm, and took out a knife that had been tucked into the waistline of her jeans. I stood frozen as she stabbed Mr. Tang in his stomach. She then ran out of the store after the other girls.

I saw Mr. Tang begin to bleed. Blood oozed from his belly. He made a loud guttural cry as he maneuvered his body with effort over to the landline behind the cash register to call 911. Moments later, for the second time in my life, I was confronted with the loud scream of an ambulance siren racing towards me. The ambulance scream was like the scream happening inside my head, which I could not let out of my mouth. This time the ambulance was coming for Mr. Tang instead of for me or my mother. As soon as the paramedics arrived, I heard a second siren which turned out to be a police siren. Two policemen came into the liquor store. One of them tried to speak to Mr. Tang as he was being treated by the paramedics. I was handcuffed and placed in the back of a patrol car.

At the police station an officer told me to call my mother, but I called Nan instead. This same officer kept asking me why I stabbed Mr. Tang, and I kept insisting I never stabbed Mr. Tang. I told him that I had no idea what was happening at the time Mr. Tang was stabbed. I said that if he didn't believe me all he had to do was to look at the video camera which Mr. Tang installed on the ceiling of his store last year. The police officer told me that he tried to look at the video footage, but the camera was not working properly. He said that unless I told him who stabbed Mr. Tang I would be taken down to Juvenile Hall for processing.

I was taken down before Nan even had time to arrive by streetcar to the police station. The one absolute truth I knew was that I would be worse off if I told the police anything about the She-Dogs. I was angry and I felt betrayed by all of them, but I believed Monica when she told me earlier that it was better to be locked up than to be labelled a snitch. Word got around about snitches. That day, before Mr. Tang got stabbed, I had no clue how dangerous the She-Dogs could be.

It took hours for Nan to come and see me. I told her I had done nothing wrong, but I was not sure she believed me, even though I was her granddaughter. I asked her if I could see my mother, and she told me that my mother was at a rehab place that did not allow phone calls or visitors for the first eight weeks of her recovery. I was assigned a public defender who came to see me the next day, but I refused to speak to her. I refused to say anything at all about the incident, other than the fact that I was innocent. I felt like Andy Dufresne in *The Shawshank Redemption*, one of Nan's most favorite movies, professing my innocence to anyone who asked. I went to mandatory summer school, went to the library every day, or stayed in my room reading books and collecting words. Unlike Monica who had been so proud to tell me about her arrest for selling drugs, I felt ashamed. I was ashamed that I caused my mother to be sent to a residential program. I was ashamed and angry that I could not help her because I was in custody. I was ashamed for hanging out with the She-Dogs.

Every time my public defender came to see me, she told me that unless I let her know exactly what happened at Mr. Tang's Liquors, she was going to have a tough time helping me get out of Juvenile Hall. She said I might even have to go to something called an out-of-home placement in Arizona rather than return to my grandmother's home. I was being charged with aiding and abetting a robbery and a serious felony assault. She said I was hurting my own case by not trusting her and by not letting her know what I did inside the store or what happened. I listened to her, rolled one of my new favorite words around in my mouth, then spit it out at her. I told her that her arguments were *specious*, that I couldn't tell her what I did at Mr. Tang's Liquors, since I didn't do anything. She said she would have to waive the ten-day time period for my trial so that she could gather some kind of evidence to defend me. She needed to prove I had nothing to do with the stabbing and robbery of Mr. Tang.

I remember that there was one night when the juvenile probation officers ordered in pizzas from Domino's Pizzeria for all of us incarcerated kids. I am not sure why we got such an unusual treat. It was the only pleasant meal during my entire stay. I continued to meet with my social worker and public defender, who both recommended to the judge that my case get transferred from the juvenile delinquency system to the dependency court system which already had an open case against my mother for neglect. I tried to understand what these different court systems were, but could only understand that one meant custody, and the other court system meant I would be free. They argued that I should be released. The judge did not agree to release me and set my case for trial in thirty days.

My public defender again came to see me to ask if I had any helpful information to give her. I told her that I was turning fifteen in ten months and that I hoped to be home by then since I was innocent and needed to take care of my mother. She said she would file a motion for my release pending trial and asked me to attend the hearing. She also told me I could say a few words on my own behalf if I wished to exercise this right. I thought long and hard about speaking, and the night before the hearing I decided I would say a few words to the judge. I needed to be careful with my words and what I chose to say so that I would not reveal the identities of the other girls.

A probation officer brought me down to court in my light green jail pants and shirt. This clothing made me extremely self-conscious. I was not looking my best in these clothes, and I wanted to look respectful when I spoke to the judge. I could see through the little window in the holding cell what was happening it the courtroom. I sat with three other girls who wore the same green clothes, and who were waiting for their own cases to be called. Sitting there was like being inside a stalled elevator. As I glanced through the window, I saw that the judge did not look his best either, which made me feel better. He was a fat white bald man wearing a billowy black robe. Although I could not hear what he was saying from inside the holding cell, I could see that when this judge did not like something one of the lawyers was telling him, his face would turn red, and his nostrils would flare like a bull.

Each case was confidential since we were juveniles. We had to wait our turn, one by one, for our matters to be called by a court officer. It seemed like I had to wait for hours. When it was finally my turn, the juvenile probation officer let me out of the holding cell and into the courtroom while my case was officially announced to the judge. The assistant district attorney looked like she was no older than the oldest of the She-Dogs. My public defender sat on the left-hand side of the courtroom with the social worker. There was a bailiff in a uniform who had handcuffs dangling on a chain from his belt. He seemed bored and kept looking at his watch. He stood to the right side of the court reporter who was typing down everything that everybody said.

When I turned and looked behind me, I could see Mr. Tang seated in the back of the courtroom. He sat with his oldest daughter. There was another woman sitting with them who I did not recognize. I sat down at the table next to my public defender and listened as she went on and on about my good grades and my gifted abilities. She spoke about my test scores and how I was testing three levels above the standard test range for my age in English proficiency. This made me want to laugh out loud. I did not see how anything about grades and test scores could ever help me get out of custody. She went on to talk about the fact that I had no prior record of arrests whatsoever, that I never left the scene of the crime, and that I did not have a knife on me when the police arrested me.

The assistant district attorney dangled pictures of Mr. Tang's injury in front of the judge. She went on and on about the seriousness of the stab wound. As she spoke, I suddenly realized that Chinese was being spoken in the back of the courtroom at the same time that anyone said anything. I figured out that the other woman next to Mr. Tang was an interpreter. I thought this was odd, since Mr. Tang always spoke to me in English whenever I came into his store.

The judge finally looked at me and asked me if there was anything I wanted him to know. My public defender bent down and whispered in my ear that I did not have to say anything. I replied back to her that I thought she wanted me to talk. She whispered in a voice loud enough for everyone in court to hear that she wanted me to talk to her, not necessarily to the whole courtroom.

I looked over at Mr. Tang, stood up and told the judge that I had something to say. I then told the judge that I was worried about my mother. I worried about her every night, and I needed to get out of custody to check on her and take care of her. I also wanted him to know how much I liked Mr. Tang. As I spoke, I looked over at the Chinese interpreter to make sure she was interpreting everything I said. I continued to tell the judge that I had lived on the same block as Mr. Tang's Liquors for just about my entire life. I liked to go to Mr. Tang's store every day to buy *muy* and coke. I told him that Mr. Tang gave me free butterscotch candy. I turned around and faced Mr. Tang directly and said,

"You remember me, don't you Mr. Tang? I would come into your store every day until I had to move to my grandmother's house. I was your best customer. Wasn't I your best customer?"

Mr. Tang then spoke to me in English, waiving off the interpreter. He said, "Yes, I know you. I see you all the time. You are always respectful to me." He turned to the judge and continued speaking. "Your honor, this girl never touched me. She never stole anything from me. It was the other girls, and not her. She always comes to my shop. She always pays. Very nice girl."

The judge's face became balloon red with anger. He shouted to both my public defender and the assistant district attorney to "approach the bench." Then he said to the court reporter "We are off the record." After that he yelled "I want to know why she was charged with a crime at all and why she's been in custody for this long."

He continued to snarl and demanded to see the District Attorney himself. The young female assistant district attorney stammered out something about me having aided and abetted the other girls who were in the store committing crimes. The judge listened to her, and when she was finally done speaking, he again demanded that she either dismiss my case right then and there or bring her supervisor down from the main office to dismiss my case. My own lawyer stood back. She was smart enough not to say anything. The judge took a break, and I was taken by the court officer back into the holding cell.

I waited for another forty minutes in the holding cell until I was finally let back out into the courtroom. I watched the young district attorney stand up at her table and announce that she was dismissing my case "in the interest of justice." She also wanted the court record to reflect that her office would consider refiling these charges if I ever committed any crimes in the future. My public defender gave me a big hug and thanked the judge as though she had won the church raffle.

We walked out of the courtroom with the bailiff. I was taken to a counter to retrieve my street clothes and then back to my room to get dressed. My social worker notified my grandmother to come and pick me up. I was handed the small change that had been taken from me when I was brought into custody. Once dressed, I sat with my public defender downstairs to wait for Nan. I knew it would take her a long time to come and pick me up from Juvenile Hall. I kept staring at the disabled ramp through the glass door, anxious for her to appear. As I waited, I thought for a while about the words that the assistant district attorney used: "dismissed in the interest of justice." I rolled the word *justice* around in my mouth, turned it over with my tongue, then let it slip to the back of my throat, right where the butterscotch candy had lodged. Sucking that word into the back of my throat near my windpipe did not make it hard for me to breath or to swallow, but as the word settled down in my gullet, I knew I might never understand its true meaning, even long after I looked it up in the dog eared Webster's dictionary I was taking home with me.

Susan M. Breall

Departures

It was my fault, I told you to leave. Said, *I think you should go*, like a woman in a made-for-TV movie. We both know I sometimes say things for the drama, just to push the buttons you claim not to have. Always so controlled, so even-keeled, the compartments of your brain so unyieldingly ordered and unbreachable. So unlike me. A thing to love and, after some time, hate.

But that night, you matched me. Huffed and grabbed your old military duffel, began shunting socks and underpants and anything inside, as I tried to relocate myself in a children's book, some part of me, even then, amid a crisis of my own creating, trying to maintain normalcy. Women's work, if ever.

When beetles fight these battles in a bottle with their paddles —

I rolled my eyes at you, yanking on drawer handles, then pivoted: *I didn't actually mean* leave *leave. Not the house. Just the room.* Backpedal, backpedal. How like me to volley the grenade while insisting I'd never planned to pull the pin.

— and the bottle's on a poodle and the poodle's eating noodles. Oh, for fuck's sake.

You stayed silent, knowing it would only make me madder, but slammed all the doors, punctuating your descent through the house and out. A marble plonked and spinning through toy pipes.

Later, in the dashboard hue of our bedroom, lit blue by the toddler's nightlight, I felt myself dimming. Was surprised to find, beneath the imprint of anger, how much I didn't feel.

Recalled times I'd used the hard, flinty fodder of our lives to write like someone in crisis. Facsimile, only.

Because here it was, the thing at which I'd hinted, in flowery, tumbling phrases meant to seem poignant and wrenching, and there was no sting, no breast beating, no hair pulling. Maybe some fear. Yes, that.

I sang the last lines of the toddler's lullaby — an old song made new about wagon wheels that I'd felt cool introducing you to, years ago. You were more of a classic rock guy, of a different generation, and my youth by comparison had felt electric, to us both, I think. I stroked the tiny mound of her, humped and foot-tucked, and finger-climbed the rungs of her perfect spine, up and down and up again. From half sleep, she asked where you were going, sensing even in her small years the wrongness of it. I kept singing. Resented not the asking, but being left to flounder. Her days were so peppered with questions, learning and mapping the world, and rare was the time I couldn't answer. Your fault. I added that to some tally I was keeping.

I waited for the slow-breathed twitch that meant full sleep and rolled carefully away. The floorboards that popped underfoot spoke, same as ever, and I thanked them for their constancy.

People gave me flack for keeping her in the bed with us, but I couldn't get close enough. Something about knowing she was our last. I would never mind her sprawl, legs and arms starfishing into the folds of our necks, our ears. We'd laughed over how such a small body could commandeer so much space. In the slice of light as I opened the door, she reached across wrinkled sheets and into the bowl still left by your head in the pillow.

I couldn't pinpoint, really, why it had started. Maybe it had been starting for longer than I'd admitted to myself. I am good at glossing over.

For years, we'd hardly argued. Or, we only ever argued about the same things, which is nearly not arguing. You would admit aggravation over my unwillingness to learn our finances and I would laugh and deflect, say something about not worrying my pretty little head, knowing we both understood my deep hatred of numbers and calculations. But I would complain when there wasn't enough, and you would grumble that if I would just learn your system... I would suggest a vacation or an outing or theater tickets or *something* and you would remind me of the septic problems last fall or the swimming pool liner or the orthodontia payments or the tree that fell precariously close to the living-room window and needed emergency maintenance which cost so much more than I ever could've imagined, though we'd both agreed the tree guy was cute and fun to watch. Rinse and repeat.

The older two, I knew, would've watched you go. Their windows faced the driveway and, even if the always too loud YouTube/TikTok/Snapchat/Minecraft drone that seeped from headphones had dulled them to your exit, they would've caught the white spill of the floodlight illumining your exit. *Staring up the road and pray to God I see headlights.*

I pulled our bedroom door shut with exaggerated care — *Look at me! The calm, responsible parent!* — but couldn't bring myself to breach their own closed doors.

I turned the shower as hot as I could stand and let it run, clouding the bathroom and something else. Impossible, I think, to overstate the curative powers of hot water. Years before, deeply pregnant and paining, the hot palm of the full tub was the only panacea. Undressing, the mirror, nearly fogged, showed a blurred body I could still be proud of. Mostly. It was a sometimes spoken half joke between us: the lopsidedness of the ages, our appearances. *How did he get her?* Just then, even my vanity felt a sham.

I was unprepared for the betrayal of spaces. The shower bore so much evidence: the rust ring left by your shaving can, where I'd asked and asked and asked you not to leave it; the shrivelled puck of seafoam soap, because you never changed your tastes; your chest and pubic hairs, curled and scattered bountifully about the drain. It would be like this now, I realized, nearly everywhere I looked. Even if you returned (and you would probably return), we would have a Before and an After.

I steamed and soaked and ruminated on dissolution. How something once so convincingly solid could corrode, grow particulate, and, unseen, begin floating away, speck by speck. Like those dandelion tattoos everyone thought were a good idea. There had been a time when we would sleep face-to-face on a sofa, so keen were we to be close. I'd told you then of a myth gleaned (sort of) from a one-off college philosophy course. The details were hazy, but the gist was there. We'd been born star-shaped — four-limbed, double-headed, hermaphroditic — only to be cleaved by an angry god on high. The half-people were left to wander, ever hoping to find the matching severed body that could make them whole, return them to their true star-shaped self. You'd held me and said, *That sounds about right.*

After, I dipped my fingers into the night cream I liked — the kind made by the local woman who forages the ingredients herself, skinning soft bark and mortaring nuts into paste, if you believe her Instagram — and stroked upward against the flesh of my neck (*still taut!*), my cheeks. More tucking, more stroking. Thought only that, with you gone, I couldn't afford another pot.

The man (boy) from the food co-op came to mind. Not the first time. He was furred about the face and long-haired, though kept it in a bun, the way men did now. He and I had joked about *letting your hair down sometime* and he'd come damn near close to winking at me. Certainly, there was a glint. He knew me by my first name and used it. Maybe this was true of all the members, but I chose to doubt it. Often, our knuckles brushed as he gave me my change. I shopped there, of course, to be able to say that I did. For the karmic brownie points. But also, and increasingly, for the frisson. My eldest had revealed recently that her friends referred to me as a MILF. I'd thrilled stupidly at this. Women arrived, it seemed, at an age when much of what they think about is trying to reclaim a moment of intoxication, something once elemental, now spent and squandered, then mourned. It was all so exhausting. What, actually, was I going to do? How did anyone do this, at this late stage in the game?

I moved from the night cream to my hair, wondering at the ease with which some things unthread. Massaged into my scalp the serum promising to thicken those thin strands and tried not to be sickened by so much trying. I was not new and shiny.

Barefoot, I summoned the closing imperative of a recent yoga class: *Breathe in and feel grounded. Feel your strong body, tethered to the earth, and trust it. You are enough.* It had felt, in class, like prescriptive rubbish. Like the kind of thing a yoga teacher says because she has to, all the while planning her locally sourced, microgreen, dressing-on-the-side lunch order and her next beige-heavy Instagram post about journaling and shared trauma. But all our sweaty, trying bodies needed to hear it. And I'm the one "liking" all the beige. I wear the $80 athleisure leggings. I buy the organic, free-range eggs and the kale I know will molder in the drawer, its leaves bleeding tawny juices until, defeated, I throw it out — *but to the compost!* — and mop out the tainted bin of my smartphone-compatible refrigerator. So, I breathed in. Pressed the mound of my big toes into the looping chenille of the bathmat. Felt myself take up space. Breathed again. These tactics maybe had their place.

I towelled, dressed, prepared to brave the doorways of the teens. They surprised me, though, and emerged as one at the sound of my own turning knob.

It was bruising to see their faces, so conditioned toward coolness, look stricken. They wore a lot of eyeliner then, always smudged, and hair fringed down past their eyes, so it was hard to tell if they'd been crying. I swept their bangs aside and knew it was bad because neither one batted my hand away. I thought, briefly, of hugging them, but that seemed too much. Maybe? He wasn't dead, just gone. It was one night.

They followed me downstairs and I could see, in the way they barely jostled each other on the steps, that they'd agreed, silently, somewhere amid the noise, to not ask. In the kitchen, though I hadn't said, one began loading the dishwasher as the other spritzed countertops. I grabbed the broom and worked around them. Strange how cohesion can leech, as if from pores, in a crisis. Our nervous systems calling out to one another, trying so hard to regulate, to cling. My children had never seemed so capable.

The air still smelled of dinner. Salmon with sauce. Cruel, that sensory stamp of what felt like another time, another life. Before. After. It had been only hours since we'd sat, in relative peace, the five of us around the tastefully distressed farmhouse table, talking about grades, homecoming, the eldest's vision appointment at the end of the week. The toddler had tossed most of her fish to the dog and I'd pretended not to see her squeezing grains of rice into the cracks of the table.

Tidying, I sometimes found, was almost as good as a hot shower. Everything put to rights and vinegar scented. Cleansed. A Band-Aid measure, I knew, but still. Band-Aids and breathwork.

We agreed to cue up a show — I can't remember, now, what it was; something with dark moody lighting, what the kids called "jump scares", and more heavy eyeliner — and I sat, straight-backed, thinking that I would be the glue, if I had to. Would melt the marrow from my bones, whisk it within me and let it bubble up from my holes, then smear us all with it. I'd make myself liminal, become a bridge of sticky, concatenating sinew. A net thrown out to catch and hold us all. I decided then, whatever happened, to never ask how you'd passed the night or where you'd gone.

On the steps up to bed, the eldest turned to me and asked, quietly, if you'd be back. I knew asking cost her something, but also that she couldn't not ask. That was her way; her nature would not allow this loose end to remain untied. Little, we'd called her Amelia Bedelia. Always so painstakingly literal. So compelled. She gets that from you. She must have known, too, that I couldn't possibly answer. But she had to ask.

The skin of my brave face pinched, despite the pricy night cream. The half-mounted stair felt a precipice. I walked up, you walked out.

I don't know. Don't worry about it. I'll take you in if he's not back.

But you'll be late getting the baby to preschool.

We'll figure it out.

So much would need "figuring out" if this stretched on. How had I grown to be so capable, in so many ways, and yet so stunted? I didn't take the trash out or put up the Christmas lights. I was flummoxed by fuse boxes and the fiddly pull-cord up to the attic. I didn't know, even, how to turn on the lawnmower. Oh, god. The entire basement! I never went down there. Had fumbled, recently, when a serviceman asked me to point him to the hot water heater. I didn't know which large metal rust-edged tank it was. I thought, *Fuck. I should really know how to balance the checkbook.*

Allison Collins

Bookends

Preserve your memories…

Rain cascades down as I climb into the back seat of our Honda CRV. It's dark, we're on the 101, halfway home to Santa Barbara from Berkeley, and my eyelids won't stay open. We left Barcelona a day ago, and I got no sleep on the planes.

Theresa, my wife, now in the driver's seat, argues with me. "I know I slept on the plane, but you know I hate driving in the dark." I lie down anyway, hoping it's the right choice.

Then the wet hum of the road and the splashing of the rain lull me to sleep.

Screeching rubber awakens me and I panic, trying to sit up. I can't escape, I'm belted in. Panting, I stiffen in the dark. Gravel explodes. I float through the air, weightless for an eternity. Slamming back down, I start tumbling, over and over, metal shrieking, glass shattering. Then I slide into a dizzying freefall. My head smacks hard. Everything goes black.

"Are you okay? …okay? …okay?" A male voice echoes through a tunnel. It's gloomy, I see no one. My head throbs, the world is upside down, on a slant.

"I don't know, I can't move." How long was I out? The crumpled roof at the bottom is jammed up into the passenger compartment, pinning me against the car seat above.

"Theresa?" I ask. Silence pierces my ears. My torso shakes. Is she alive? A siren splits the air. No sensation in my legs.

Smelling gas and smoke, I hear a drip.

"Where's my wife?" I scream this time. Footsteps crunch on gravel outside the door. No one answers. Blackness creeps in, stillness swallows me.

*

One week earlier: We're on vacation in Barcelona with our daughter, Sinead, for her college graduation present. At our Airbnb we meet up with two previous members of 'Reel on the Ha'Penny', my Irish traditional folk music group. Emily, the flute player, is getting her MBA at the University of Barcelona, and Kirsten, the fiddler, has flown in from Iowa, where she now lives. Sinead, the original singer/flutist, hugs her ex-bandmates. They both congratulate Sinead on her BA in Theater from UC Berkeley.

Theresa winks at me; we're in our happy zone. We save like demons for vacation so we can recharge our relationship while traveling together. Having Sinead with us is a plus. Conceived on Christmas Eve in a moment of drunken ecstasy, Sinead's happier than most anyone I know. We love being around her, even as we worry about paying her student loans.

That night we have tapas at Sebastien's apartment. Emily says he's a friend, but he's obviously more than that from their touches and eye contact. Taller, he sports a goatee and mustache. The place is macho: dark furniture, hardwood floors, leather-bound books, a wine cabinet, sexy Marvin Gaye tunes. He has us take our shoes off, but he keeps his slippers on.

As Emily serves us mouthwatering pintxos, garlic-drenched gambas, and spicy paella, Sebastien recites the recipe for each dish, like he's Jacques Pepin on TV. I'm not a big fan of foodies who toot their own horn. So I drink lots of

Tempranillo, the Spanish pinot noir, staining the yellow tablecloth while I mull over Sebastien's relationship with my friend Emily.

During dinner Emily explains her MBA project: Spanish sparkling wine in a can.

"Canned wine, who the hell's buying that?"

Sebastien jumps on my comment. "I think many people will. And I am Emily's faculty advisor. It is a practical product, less costly and less polluting. We call it *Cava in a Can*."

That raises my eyebrows. He's dating his student? Not good. Darkly handsome, he's easily ten years older than Emily. He needs to pick on somebody his own age.

"Each team designs the product, with marketing and advertising campaigns and a business plan to tie it all together," he says.

An unpaid internship is what it sounds like.

As he takes the last bit of paella, he smirks at me. "So, you play Irish nostalgia music?"

That's a jab. I look at Emily, wondering where that phrase came from. Then I look back at Sebastien. "It's the music of my ancestors, part of who I am." I wonder if my being an Irish musician tempts people to make fun of me.

Sebastien says, "The Portuguese have a word for that. *Saudade*: the homesickness of missing something from a bygone era. You, Mr. Paddy, live in the past."

He's definitely poking me, like he wants to start something.

Emily interrupts him. "Sebastien can't wait to show you Barcelona tomorrow."

I can certainly wait and I'm not willing to let his comments go. "I'm good at what I do because I'm relentless. I make sure my band performs the best they can on stage."

"Is that true?" Sebastien asks. "I haven't heard your music."

He says it like he assumes we're no good. My stomach starts churning. "Well, maybe we can get a gig here in Barcelona and show you."

Sebastien says to Emily, "I know Martin at 'The Quiet Man' pub. I can get you booked over there."

Emily looks at me. I smile and nod. So she nods at Sebastien.

"I'll book it," Sebastien says.

Now we're getting somewhere. We'll show Mr. Professor.

Sebastien turns to Kirsten and asks why she likes Irish music.

As Sinead and Theresa talk across the table, Emily turns to me, lowers her voice, and asks, "How's Sinead doing?"

"Bringing her straight to Barcelona from graduation wasn't the best idea I've had."

"You always push the envelope," Emily says. She's five years older than Sinead and is used to my hard-charging tactics with the band. I'll do most anything to engage the audience.

"I'm trying to set an example for Sinead, so she knows what it takes to succeed."

"You tell me I'm a role model for Sinead, yet you constantly push me, introducing tunes I've never seen before and making me sight-read them on the spot. You need to chill. We don't all live on the edge like you. If I'm a role model for Sinead, the only thing she's gonna learn from me is how to ignore you."

I always rush the tempo, stomp my foot, and swing my guitar like a sword on stage, trying to get the band to match my intensity and bring the audience into the urgency I feel when I perform. It's life or death for me. Without it I wouldn't know how to live.

"She's the only child I'll ever have." As if that justifies my behavior.

"And you're the only dad she'll ever have. She needs to balance the good she remembers about you against the bad." That hurts.

Emily crawls under my skin whenever she analyzes me. Not for the first time I question how we stay friends. She's religious, I'm not. She's nice, I'm a PITA — a pain in the ass. She corrects me regularly, just like she does her own dad. But I love them all: Sinead more Irish, a brunette with buttermilk skin; Emily more burnished with her mom's Filipino genes and jet-black hair; Kirsten is blond, a monster fiddle player with a dynamite sense of humor, so funny. They're very sure of themselves.

Sebastien raises his glass. "I'm glad you could all join me here."

Theresa smiles at him. "How long did it take you to cook this delicious food?"

"I cooked the food," Emily says.

Sebastien's face reddens. "I chose the recipes."

Emily snorts.

Now we're having fun. I give Sebastien a big smirk.

"You're not very humble," Theresa says.

"Someone has to take charge." Sebastien frowns, his forehead creasing.

I look over at Emily. "Is he like this in class when a student challenges him?"

"It doesn't matter who cooked, so long as everyone likes the food." Emily plays peacemaker and pours me some more wine.

Sebastien glares at me. "When students misbehave, I punish them."

That's a threat. I stand up to leave. "Well, we need to rehearse if we're going to play this gig."

❁

The next day we hike Barcelona at a military pace while pedantic Sebastien provides running commentary, just like at dinner. His low-pitched voice is seductively annoying. "And here we have Gaudi's ethereal cathedral, La Sagrada Familia."

A visual symphony of color streams through the stained-glass windows. Dense reds, vibrant blues, and rich yellows pour into the nave, a vision of paradise at sunset. The spires resemble palm trees drenched in rainbows.

Theresa says, "I've never seen colors this beautiful."

Seeing the world through her eyes grabs my heart. We clench hands.

Next, during the *Barri Gotic* tour of the original Roman city, we walk on raised platforms above subterranean ruins. Chipped stone columns, crumbling walls, and mosaic tile floors fill my eyes as Sebastien says, "These are the most extensive Roman ruins in the world."

"That can't be true. The Colosseum in Rome is much bigger." Where is he coming from?

As we leave the ruins, he claims Barcelona was named for Hannibal's father: Hamilcar Barca. He behaves like an obnoxious uncle showing off his secret font of knowledge.

Las Ramblas, Spain's most famous street, smacks my senses. A mile-long promenade as wide as a boulevard, it overflows with tourists, flower stalls, beggars, pets in cages, dancers, musicians, and street actors. People eat at white-tablecloth restaurants, food trucks, and ice cream carts.

Cellists imitate Pablo Casals, violins waft Roma music, and drummers hammer out dance rhythms. There are Africans dressed as ten-foot-tall, gold-painted dragons with huge wings and foot-long fingernails, mimes mimic a locked room, and an ancient Galileo pushes his telescope on a handcart.

As we walk Kirsten blurts outs, "I decided to join y'all in Barcelona after arguing with my boyfriend. I'm ready to marry and he's iffy. I told him I'm gonna live my life whether he wants me or not." She scowls. "He has commitment-phobia. If he doesn't marry me soon, I'm moving back to Santa Barbara."

I turn to Emily and silently ask the same marriage question about her and Sebastien.

"Don't ask," she says.

"I'd love to have you and Kirsten back in the band," I say.

Emily smiles and playfully punches me in the shoulder. I'm glad we've reconnected.

The Boqueria Market, dated 1217 and large as a football field, sports a stained-glass arch, a metal roof, and wild varieties of food and spice: live eels and monkfish and lobster; strings of garlic and chilies; rustic breads and cheeses; hanging ducks and roasted black pigs. Aromas of saffron, sardines, and deep-fried anchovies float through the barbeque smoke.

Sebastien has us stand waiting for thirty minutes to eat at El Quim, according to him the best food counter in the market. Afterward he says, "I wish they served *Cava in a Can*."

He just won't let up. I shake my head.

Sebastien says, "I notice you disagree with some of my statements."

"We can agree to disagree. But do you ever get tired of giving your opinions?"

He glares at me. "My opinions, as you call them, are a big help to Emily in her classes."

Theresa frowns as if to say, 'I bet that's not all he helps her with.' I love her nonverbal opinions.

Sebastien leaves us. On the way back to our Airbnb, I ask Emily, "What do you see in Sebastien?"

She hesitates a long minute. "He makes me feel better about myself."

Sinead interjects, "Dad, everyone has their reasons for loving someone."

"I love your father 'cause he makes me laugh," Theresa says. Everyone laughs.

When Theresa took me "for better or worse," I thought it was a miracle.

Here in Barcelona I hoped Sinead would benefit from seeing Emily and Kirsten successfully navigating life and learning how to grow — as musicians and as humans. Hearing what Kirsten had to say about her waffling boyfriend is bound to have an impression on Sinead. But I'm not happy about Emily's older professor. I wonder what else I'll learn on this trip.

✳

Friday night arrives fast. We're at the end of our vacation, only one more day in Barcelona. The pub is named after the John Wayne-Maureen O'Hara movie *The Quiet Man*. It's just off Las Ramblas, decorated in the imported Irish pub style of old farmhouse butter-churns and spinning wheels, a fake tin ceiling, and signs saying *No Irish Need Apply*. Martin, the curly-haired manager, speaks Irish-inflected English.

Customers slowly arrive but eventually we have a full house. Emily's classmates sprinkle the pub. Regulars fill the rest of the room. For some reason Sebastien wears a backpack, wandering around buying drinks and telling people what he thinks.

We start out mid-tempo with jigs and songs, and then segue to up-tempo reels with Sinead doing the Riverdance slam-bang step-dancing. Soon everyone is clapping along, pounding the tables, whistling, and drinking up a storm. I'm bouncing on my toes.

Sebastien appears to resent us doing so well and tries to imitate Sinead. He dances oafishly, like a drunken seal on sand. The regulars point at him and laugh. He deserves it.

We play some slip jigs next, and I make the mistake of swirling around and catching Emily's violin bow with the neck of my guitar. I almost take her right arm off as I yank her bow away from her violin. Luckily I don't break any arms or bows.

Sinead sings "Down by the Salley Gardens." She delivers the sad and plaintive lyric with clenched fists and fiery eyes. *He bid me take life easy, as the grass grows on the weirs.* Her powerful voice rips into everyone's heart, twisting and pulling, stroking their emotions. The audience loves her; their applause descends like rain. We can still find what we're looking for, no matter how long it's been since we've played together.

I spot Theresa snapping a photo, her eyes tearing. Mommy loves her daughter.

But then everything gets weird. Sebastien comes over to the side of the stage and turns down the PA system. He walks back to the tables, pulling cans out of his backpack.

The MBA students go in twos and threes to the tables of non-students, distributing flyers with advertising slogans on them and opening a can for each table. They produce plastic cups and offer everyone a taste of their *Cava in a Can*. Then they give a list of questions to each customer to answer, completely interrupting us as they attempt a marketing survey in the middle of our performance. Everyone starts talking over the band.

Martin raises his arms at me like, 'What the hell?'

I look over at Emily and realize she didn't know this was going to happen. No wonder Sebastien said he'd get us this gig. I should have sensed he was up to something. What an asshole. He's trying to punish me.

The regulars are yelling at the MBA students. They aren't remotely interested in being used as a test audience. Sweat drips down my arm. This isn't good.

Martin strides over, fuming. "Feckin' hell, what're you doing to my customers?"

Emily says, "Sorry, those are my MBA classmates. Sebastien must've thought this would be a good place to survey our test product."

Martin glares at me and Emily. He's pissed. He calls Sebastien over and tells him to stop doing the survey.

Sebastien says, "You have no idea. Customers love getting free champagne."

"Bollocks, you lied to me. Pack up. You're all fired, get the hell out of here." Martin looks like he might punch Sebastien. That sounds like a plan.

To have such an incredible performance and then to be fired is like falling into an abyss. We've accomplished so much, engaging the audience, playing our hearts out, and now this. Sebastien and Martin continue arguing.

Leaving, I tell Sebastien, "Your opinions certainly didn't help Emily today."

He flips me off. What else can go wrong?

❁

Pain stabs my head as I blink against the bright lights. My right leg jumps. My head is stuck, clamped by a brace under my chin. A needle is shoved in between the knuckles on my right hand, and a monitor is clipped to my left index finger. My body aches all over. Closing my eyes causes a swooping sensation. Don't know what city I'm in or what happened to Theresa.

The door opens. A smiling nurse walks in, thirty-something, brown hair in a bun.

"You're awake," she says. "How do you feel?"

"Pain… Where's my wife?" Lysol stinks the place up.

"The doctor will be here in a minute." She leaves quickly, skirting through a beam of sunlight, closing the door silently. Birds chatter outside.

I wipe my nose with the back of my left hand and it's all wet. Crying, I still know nothing about Theresa. A gray, wrinkled doctor walks in, holding his glasses.

"I'm Doctor Stevenson. Glad to see you're awake. Can you tell me your name?"

"Patrick Flaherty." How in hell can he not know my name?

"It's Tuesday, Patrick, you've been here for two days."

"Cut the crap. Where's my wife?"

"Your daughter will be here in a minute."

"You called Sinead? Where are we?"

"Cottage Hospital, Santa Barbara."

"What's going on with Theresa? Why won't anybody talk to me?"

"We thought it best if your daughter were here."

"So my wife's dead, right?" My brain feels like it's gonna burst.

The nurse walks in with Sinead crying on her shoulder. "Oh, Dad, I'm so sorry." She comes over, falls on the bed, and hugs me. I'm such a useless parent.

But I finally have my answer about Theresa. I can't remember if the first stage of grief is denial or shock or just being pissed off. I'm definitely feeling all three. From the high of Barcelona and Sinead's graduation, I'm now so hollow — the worst feeling of my life. And I can't really let go or lash out or scream. Sinead must feel as broken as I do. Her body heaves and her tears wet the hospital gown where her head is buried in my chest. Your child is always your first priority. I have to protect her.

Doc Stevenson stares at me. I assume he's trying to tell if there's something wrong with my reaction to the news, if my brain's screwed up. His name reminds me of Juliet Stevenson in that movie where her boyfriend, Alan Rickman, died and came back as a ghost to relieve her suffering. She eventually had to stop seeing him so she could claw her way back to reality.

Theresa will not be coming back as a ghost. But that doesn't mean I'll make it back to reality; I'm just fumbling at life.

No way should I be thinking about a movie when my wife is dead and our child is crying on my chest. Now I openly cry with her, shaking both our bodies. My gut twists like a noose. Doc Stevenson nods his head like I'm exhibiting appropriate behavior.

"We'll leave you two alone for a while." They exit.

He must be talking about me behind that door. How I don't have a clue. Don't know what to do about my dead wife, about healing, going back to work, overcoming grief. Nine million thoughts pour through my mind. I didn't deserve Theresa, Sinead, or the life I was allowed to live, and now this. Every minute takes an hour to pass.

As I hold Sinead in my arms, I feel I'm dying. My whole life passes in front of me. I'm flying, looking down on the past. We were so young when we met. I see the sway of her body, the shape of her hips in her bikini. We're floating on inner tubes in the Big Sur River, drifting down to the Pacific Ocean. Then, further back, the post office and meeting Theresa, not believing a happy watercolor artist could be interested in me.

Eventually we married, honeymooned in Ireland, and Sinead was born. Theresa inherited her mom's house and our life changed dramatically.

And now I'm the weary loner, inheriting that same, empty house from my dead wife.

I'm only a couple years from retirement, but I don't see how I'll make it if my heart doesn't heal. I spend the night bawling into my pillow.

Sinead is my only reality. I vow to myself I'll take care of her, no matter what.

❋

The next day is marginally better. At least I don't want to kill myself. The nurse lets in a deputy sheriff, who says he needs to interview me about the accident. He has wide black sideburns, like Elvis.

"I'm sorry for your loss, I know losing your wife is horrific, but I need to ask some questions." He's not smiling.

"Whatever." Nothing matters now that she's dead.

"Do you remember anything about the accident?"

"Hardly. I was asleep in the back with my seat belt on. When I woke the tires were howling, then we crashed and went airborne, spinning, and we landed hard and I blacked out."

"You were found upside down, screaming for your wife. Did you know anything at that point?"

"Nothing about my wife until the doc told me yesterday."

"You didn't see the BMW that pulled out in front of you?"

"No." So some rich asshole put an end to us. I'll never see Theresa again.

"There's no indication that your wife was speeding. Do you know if she'd been drinking or taking drugs?"

"She only takes prescription drugs. She had a glass of wine at dinner on the plane, but that was like twelve hours earlier."

"The autopsy will confirm that."

Jesus Christ. "Do they have to cut her open?"

"It's the law, sorry. And the BMW driver also died. He was over the legal limit for alcohol."

"Fuck him."

"He has no heirs, no wife or kids, and he owns a house on San Marcos Pass. I can't give you legal advice, but you might want to consult an attorney. You could get some money out of this."

"Blood money, it won't bring Theresa back." Nothing will.

"No, but it could make your life easier, or your daughter's life."

After a few more questions I don't know the answers to, he leaves.

In that moment it hits me: My life has changed forever.

The last number of years I've lived day-to-day, holding my breath and trying to enjoy the longest stretch of time when I've been reasonably happy. I knew I didn't deserve the happiness I'd found. I also knew it wouldn't last. I'd avoided thinking about what would happen when it ended and how I would have to find something to replace it.

That time has come. I need to go to the edge again and grab the reins of the next dream. "You need a plan," I hear — or seem to hear — the ghost of Theresa say, close by my ear. "Sinead will only understand a plan." It's almost like the Juliet Stevenson movie.

Sinead comes back in as I try to reimagine my future. "How are you feeling, Dad?" Her wistful smile matches her sad tone.

"I'm okay, babe. Just trying to take it all in. I'm not prepared for any of this."

"I know, I feel lost. But I have to go back to Berkeley soon, rehearsal on *The Tempest* starts next week." I forgot she was doing San Francisco Shakespeare Festival for the summer. "Have you thought about what we need to do for Mom: funeral, burial, anything?"

"No, I've just been lying here feeling sorry for myself. And for you."

"I didn't live with her. It's going to be much harder for you."

Got to watch what I say. Need to stay on an even keel. "Did you talk to the sheriff?"

"No, what did he say?"

I relate the crash story. "None of that helps us now. We'd much rather have Mom back, but I can't lie here and do nothing, it'll kill me." *Think, think.* "Will you call the company that cremated Grandma Kitty, that Neptune Society, and try and get someone to come here with the contracts? At least we'll get that rolling. I'm gonna get the name of a lawyer who can sue the drunk's estate. See what kind of money we can get out of it. If I can get enough to pay your student loans, we'll at least feel something good came out of this."

"You should do something for yourself, you lost Mom."

"We both lost her." But if I focus on Sinead, if I have someone living to focus on, I won't think about Theresa's death every two minutes.

"When are they letting you out of here?"

"The nurse said I could go home tomorrow." The last place I want to be by myself.

"I can stay with you for a couple more days. Then I have to leave. Think about what sort of celebration we should do for Mom's life." Her eyes well up; she's starting to cry again.

"I can't do anything right now. Let's talk after your Shakespeare Festival is over."

"Okay, I'll call those Neptune people and come get you tomorrow." She kisses me. "Love you."

❁

One year later the lawsuit is finally resolved, giving me a cash windfall that I use to pay off Sinead's student loans — finally something positive.

When I show up in Berkeley to talk to Sinead, I'm breathing heavily, lightheaded. I'm not a stage father like Michael Jackson's dad, and I know nothing about getting agents, directors, or producers interested in Sinead's career. I need to run my plan by her.

We have dinner before her performance in *Trojan Women* at the Aurora Theater. Sinead dresses classy in a sleek black pantsuit and pumps. I look like a vagrant in an old polo and jeans.

Over salmon she says, "This may come as a shock, but I'm dating James, the director of the play." She looks down at her plate and laughs. "We each thought we were only ten years apart, but it turns out he's actually fifteen years older than me." She shrugs like it's no big deal. A shiver runs down my back. This is not the behavior I wanted her to emulate.

How do I broach my idea? "I'm…I'm thinking of moving to the Bay Area and helping with your career."

She almost drops her water glass. "Helping how?"

"I don't know, getting you an agent, doing promotion, marketing, something. I feel like I'm just spinning my wheels in Santa Barbara."

"That won't work." She frowns. "I'm in charge of my own career."

Exhale. Now I'm frustrated. My hope of going to the edge and riding along on her dream crashes. I put my left hand over my right to stop it from shaking. We'd each lost someone — a wife, a mother, a friend. And now we're losing each other.

Everything I see on my way back to the hotel room intensifies my anger: happy people, nice cars, crowded restaurants. It all seems full of stupidity. Berkeley pisses me off.

I crawl back to Santa Barbara, despondent, and resume my county IT job, plugging the holes in my life by rebuilding the band. I'm hiding from my fears.

It's a no-brainer to pay for Kirsten to move back to Santa Barbara from Iowa. She works as the West Coast rep for Cremona violins and drives our performances at Beckett's Irish Pub.

Emily finishes her MBA at the University of Barcelona, comes home to Santa Barbara. She apologizes, telling me Sebastien is out of her life, and rejoins the band.

But I've not remotely recovered. I lie to my therapist about understanding my grief.

And all the while I'm on cruise control, a zombie robot during the day, slightly more animated at night with the band, while existing on fast food, paper plates, shit sleep, and pinot noir. The alcohol blunts the pain. Still, my whole body aches. The dark hours are the worst.

Unable to sleep tonight, I sit in my empty living room, staring out the window, guitar in hand. I strum a minor blues chord, letting the melancholy notes fill the room, matching the drizzle outside in the gloom — the same atmosphere as the night of the accident. The echo evokes that dark memory, coloring my dread. A cramped, airless feeling clutches my chest, closes off my future. I'm trying hard to understand the death of Theresa and the loss of a closer relationship with my daughter.

The "nostalgic" Irish music I perform with the other two girls, both of whom are recovering from their own lost relationships, is my only creative outlet.

There's the photograph on the coffee table — a happy memory, taken by Theresa — of the band performing at 'The Quiet Man'. We're all smiles right before the marketing disaster happened. It's a fleeting moment in time that can't be recovered or relived.

But I cradle Theresa's memory.

As the drizzle picks up, I try not to be overwhelmed by the homesickness of missing the past: *Saudade*. I'm evolving but not necessarily gaining intelligence.

My chest pulses, sucking in air. I can't accept Theresa's death. I can't. My other half has been ripped away. Her face is slipping from memory.

The scary part is I never know when I'll burst into tears.

How many times can I tell her I'm sorry? We never even got to say goodbye.

My mind drifts up to the ceiling, looks back down. Theresa would laugh to see me pitying myself.

She once said, "If I die before you, remember me, then move on and find love."

Today she'd say, "Stop romanticizing your pain. Get on with life."

I swear I'll listen to her.

The rains stills. A pale soup of moonlight filters through the branches outside.

Russell Doherty

Teacher of the Year

"Did you have a question, Emily?" *Of course, she has a question.*

"Mr. Brooks, can you explain what this experiment is supposed to teach us about science?" Emily was the kind of seventh grader who took notes on everything. She waited anxiously for my answer with her pencil resting under the word 'Goal' on a blank sheet of paper.

"Sure." I took off my glasses, rubbed my eyes, and stepped in front of the projector screen.

"And is there going to be a test?" Julien interrupted from the back of the class, clueless and disruptive, as always.

"We're going to grow mushrooms. So, to answer your question, Emily, we're going to learn about the different parts of mushrooms, the conditions under which they grow, and the role they play in ecosystems. That's science."

"Hmmm," she said, unconvinced, looking down at her blank paper. "But our next section in the textbook is supposed to be about the scientific method."

"Yeah, well, textbooks are schools' way of making sure you don't enjoy what you learn."

"But I read the textbook," Emily said.

"I'm sure you do," I said with a smirk. "But you can put it away."

Julien gave a quick "woohoo, no test!" from the back and slammed his book shut.

I could tell the class was a little surprised at how miserable I looked. My eyes felt like sad drapes from a deserted house, and my five o'clock shadow made me look like I had been in an asylum against my will. Rogue strands of my short, curly hair stuck out at random around my head and ears, but I didn't care.

"Another thing you should know is that these aren't just any mushrooms. College kids and phony spiritual healers call them magic mushrooms. They have a chemical in them called psilocybin, which makes you hallucinate when you eat them." Julien eyes grew big — I could tell he was paying attention for the first time this year. "We're going to grow them, and then I'm going to sell them because they're worth a lot of money. So, if it helps, it's a lesson in science and economics. And it's really important that if anyone, either in school or out, asks about what you are doing, you don't tell them. Just say you're learning about the environment."

The class was silent, expecting me to back out and rethink my decision. Fat chance. "Ok, Darius, can you come up and grab the bin here so we can prepare the compost? We're going to go over the different parts of the mushroom, then plant our spawn. Once they're planted, we sit back and watch them grow, which will take about a month."

"And they just pop up out of nowhere?" Julien said.

"Not out of nowhere, they grow because of their environment, and their environment grows because of them."

The class thought about what I said. I noticed Emily in the front row writing "Because of the environment," then I turned around to get the Ziploc bag of mushroom spawn off my desk.

❄

A month before I kicked off the experiment with my class, my wife Casey left me. We had only been married a year when I came home from getting club soda and bread at the store on New Year's Day. She was holding a glass of wine, standing beside her champagne-colored rolling luggage bag, and biting her lower lip. "Well, Marshall. You just aren't…you aren't ambitious enough," she said as if she was describing a regrettable liver condition. She told me that one of her New Year's goals was to be more comfortable — comfortable meant rich. She patted me on the shoulder, worried that too much affection might give me the wrong idea, and then told me I had until the summer to move out of our house. Since that day, I've felt like I imagine most men in my position do — ashamed and alone. I wished I was charismatic enough to go out and fill the void with sex. I'm also furious at her for letting us waste our twenties (and all my money) on a relationship she obviously felt was wrong from the beginning.

"Ok, everyone, today we're going to check on our mushrooms and talk about their role in ecosystems," I told the class. A diagram of the water cycle hung behind me on the blackboard. A poster pinned to the back wall had the word "Science" written in letters made from the periodic table. My voice hung low as I spoke. My depression had turned into a newfound nihilism — luckily, they couldn't feel my hangover.

"What is a substrate again?" Julien asked, kicking off the lesson for me.

"That is the soil where the mushrooms grow. They need a nutrient source just like we do." I turned around and picked up a small leaf-shaped Rye Berry on my desk to hold it up. "Does everyone remember this?"

"Uh huh," Emily said. "It's what we planted a couple of weeks ago. It's the mushroom spawn." Emily sat up a little straighter, confident that this was the correct answer.

"That's right. If you all remember, these little grains were injected with mushroom spores so the mushroom could spawn and colonize. Then we added the colonized...does anyone remember the word?"

"Myclum?" Jackson, a reserved boy whose voice cracked when he spoke, said.

"Mycelium, right? Remember all the little white threads we saw when we put it in the compost? Pretty cool. Why doesn't everyone grab their notebook and gather around our garden tub up front? We're going to document our observations like good scientists."

I unzipped the indoor growing station I bought from the hardware store. Inside were two clear tubs of compost with at least fifty different mushrooms sticking out — some just a quarter of an inch, some closer to three — above the dark bottom layer. The caps were burnt orange and brown with thin stems — like tiny umbrellas for a caterpillar.

"If you look closely, there is a caterpillar with a hookah underneath," I said dryly.

No one laughed. The kids in the back stood on their toes to see while the whole class leaned in. There was a chorus of "ahhhs."

"I thought plants needed sunlight," Jackson said.

"Not the case with mushrooms. They like the dark. They are kind of like the friend that does nothing but hang out in his parents' dark basement, eating Cheetos and playing video games. Then, one day, he comes out and starts a biotech company."

"Cool," Julien said, no doubt because of the reference to video games.

Emily stepped forward first, touching the top of one of the mushrooms to see if it was real, while Jamie looked over her shoulder. The class took turns checking them out from the front of the rough circle. I checked to make sure the piece of blue construction paper was still covering the window into my room so my principal could not peek in.

"Get a good look. Notice all the tiny white hairs that have grown in the compost. The mushrooms above the ground are only one part of the fungus. They are the fruit."

"I don't like the word fungus," Emily said. Julien and Darius laughed in the back.

"Mungus!" Darius yelled, and the class all chuckled.

"Alright everyone, quiet down. Does anyone know why mushrooms, actually fungi, are so important to ecosystems?"

Emily looked at Jamie, but neither knew, so they stayed silent. I beamed with mischievous pride — a genuine teaching moment. Too bad I had stopped caring about my job.

"They are a part of a class of living things called decomposers. The decomposers don't typically get much attention — you'll never see them at a zoo or on a postcard — but they're vital to life on Earth. Does anyone know why?"

"Sounds like a band." Julien half-yelled from the back, clueless but sometimes endearing.

"Sure, nice observation, Julien. They aren't a grunge band, though. Anyone else want to venture a guess?"

"They take stuff apart?" Emily said, looking up at me from the front row.

"Kind of. Decomposers, like our fungi, find dead material like leaves, plants, old trees, or even animals, and they recycle all the matter those things have into nutrients for other plants. The other plants suck up the nutrients through their roots, like a milkshake."

The class looked at me with blank stares. Outside, a whistle from a gym class blew.

"They take something that has died and help create a new life." Suddenly, I was struck by the thought of my recently dissolved marriage. I got distracted by kids yelling for the soccer ball outside.

"I don't understand," Emily's hand went up.

I explained further, going into detail about what nutrients fungi usually provide. Then, I gave them examples of how many fungi there are on the Earth. The class could tell it was a rare moment of excitement for me in the middle of what had been a string of apathetic lectures lately. What surprised me most about the conversation was that the kids were the ones who made the connection between fungi and humans' knack for reinvention — I didn't prompt them at all. It was Jackson who spoke up and said "Huh, kind of like people," after I commented that nothing really dies because of fungi when you think about it. They all loved it — their eyes were as wide as dinner plates. Emily even knelt and tried to peer up on the mushrooms from below the tub. The willingness to be amazed is such an admirable quality; adults really should look into it.

＊

One day, I got an email from Casey with a subject line that read, "Just letting you know…".

Before reading it, I walked to the kitchen to get an old Coors light out of the fridge that now held only condiments. There wasn't much furniture left in the house except for my old college recliner with a hole in the arm and my hand-me-down desk, which had ornate wooden legs like something from Victorian England. I cracked the beer, took a long gulp, and sat at my monitor to read.

"You're going to find out eventually," it started. "…so I figured I might as well tell you. I moved in with Owen. Don't tell any of my friends. Not like you talk to them anyway. But things are just so easy, you know. It's nice not having the drama we always had — me always on your case about going back to school. Anyway, now you know. Oh, that feels so much better. By the way, this doesn't mean I don't still want you out of the house. Please don't take it the wrong way."

Owen was a rich, entitled, blowhard acquaintance from high school who lived nearby. He worked part-time as a Tennis instructor, living off his parents' money, because he wasn't sure he had found the career fit — what an asshole. How could I take it the wrong way?

Back in class, it was time to harvest.

"Alright, everyone, it's a big day. Today, we harvest our first batch of mushrooms." I said, bringing my lanky arms together with a clap. The class could tell that my excitement was a poor attempt to convince myself I wasn't depressed, but I pressed on undeterred.

I looked the room over. Jackson sat at a desk on the side of the class, drawing mushroom sketches in his spiral notebook with his head down. Emily rubbed her hands together in anticipation — it made me laugh that she was excited about something illegal.

"What are we going to do after we harvest?" Julien said from the back.

"We're going to dry them with this industrial fan over here that I borrowed from the school." I held out my hand to show an old metal clunker to my left. "Then we're going to package them up in Ziploc bags."

"So, what do these things do again if you eat them?" Jamie asked.

"Well, it depends on how much you eat. For some people, it makes them hallucinate — that means to see things that aren't really there."

"Whoaa," Jackson said, looking up from his drawing.

"Like, could I hallucinate Alicia Silverstone naked?" Darius yelled.

"Eeeewwww!" Jamie screeched.

I ignored the comment, then waved my hand to tell everyone to get out of their seats and come up to our bin. I walked back to my desk to get the tiny scissors.

"Who wants to do the honors?" I held them up for everyone to see.

Emily took a step forward, and I handed them down. The kids all huddled around her as she walked up to the tub. I lifted the plastic lid as she peeked in — it was covered with our little seventh-grade experiment in subversion. Emily looked to me for direction.

"All you have to do is snip the mushroom at the stem, right above the compost. Then take it out and put it on the drying rack over here. Don't worry everyone, you'll all get a chance to do it."

One by one, they took turns while I watched with the satisfaction of sharing something authentic — way better than memorizing the scientific method.

A moment later, my principal poked his head into my room. I jumped when I turned around to look at the partially open door.

"Marshall, a word, please. In my office," he said with his eyebrows raised.

"Uh, yeah, sure." My palms began to sweat. "Just go ahead and read the next chapter, everyone." They laughed, not even bothering to leave the circle around the growing station.

I arrived at the frosted glass door that led to my principal's office, which read "Franklin 'Frankie' Thornbloom, Principal" on the front — no one called him Frankie.

"Come on in Marshall. How are you today?" he said, reclining in his tall leather chair as I stepped in slowly.

"I've been better." I sat down, preparing to recite all the content from the standard seventh-grade science curriculum I was teaching.

"Well, everyone has bad days," Frank said dismissively. "Look, it has come to my attention that you are teaching some sort of experiment that isn't in the curriculum?"

"It's a science class, Frank. Experiments are pretty standard," I said, hoping a short answer and a bit of bluster would scare him off.

"Huh," he said as if pondering if my statement had merit. "Yeah, well, it shouldn't be interesting or fun or anything like that. Teachers always think they can outsmart the system and make learning fun. Just make the little maniacs learn so they can take their tests."

I hated this guy. "I will, don't worry."

He looked at me and thought for an awkward moment in silence. I straightened my short-sleeved, plaid, collared shirt and readjusted myself in my chair. He was trying to decide if he could trust me.

"I've got it, Frank. Don't worry about it." I said, surprising myself at how confident I sounded.

"Well…if I found out you were doing something like going off and teaching them how to grow pot, I would have to come down on you. I can't have that on my school's record. Even though you seem like an ok teacher."

"Of course. Nothing like that." I said, nodding in complete agreement. I looked at him as he sized me up. He tapped his Bic against the table, looking at a sheet of paper with a list of the recommended seventh-grade science topics. I understood then how this would end and why it was necessary. Difficulties give us the nudge we need to rethink our lives, which is what I had to do, even if it meant starting over.

"Says here they should be learning about the scientific method. Then atoms and molecules?"

"We will, Frank. Can I go now?"

"Yeah, sure."

Walking back to my class, through the halls with spirit day flyers, I had a strange expression. It came from that self-destructive impulse that makes you want to jump off a ledge that you know is just a little too high to be safe. I also just wanted to prove to myself I could be interesting.

❋

Casey and I met at a party in college. I loved her laugh; that was what did it. When she heard a joke, she would blurt out an awkward, 'Ha!'. You could never tell if she was making fun of you or laughing sincerely. I hadn't heard that laugh since college though. We got out, and both got jobs: she opted for a high-powered finance role working fifteen-hour days, and I chose to be a middle-school science teacher. She lost the ability to see past the self-inflicted, masochistic pressures of adult life — the constant nagging voice telling you need a bigger house, a new car, and a professionally manicured yard to be happy. I wonder if Casey's child will have that laugh. That would be great; the world needs it.

Weeks after the harvest, I was eating my cold pasta from a Tupperware in the faculty break room when I heard whistles and hollers from the hall. Our gym teacher, Ben Stickler, went out first. I didn't think much of it because he was always first to try and keep the kids in line, so I kept chatting with our music teacher, Melissa Grey, about how they needed a Tuba player for their recital. Then we both heard a loud crack, like a door had been busted down, and our heads whipped toward the door.

We left our meals and walked out to the locker commons. The locker commons had an open space in the middle, with rows of lockers forming the perimeter. There was a barricade in the middle where the lockers stopped. Desks had been piled high on top of one another to give the kids in the center a space where no one could get to them. They were playing electronic music really loud from a portable speaker and dancing. Mr. Stickler was trying to remove the desks and chairs to extract the kids.

This wasn't even the most surprising thing I saw. As I looked across the commons, I noticed all the kids wandering around without any real direction. Some were lying in the middle of the floor. Jason Lewis and Dave McCaferty had removed their shirts and climbed the steel supports over the lockers like they were on a playground. Jess Burndon, a cerebral girl who usually walked around with her face in a fantasy novel, was sitting, legs crossed in the middle of the hall, tearing pages out of a textbook and making paper airplanes. I watched two girls with a lighter start a campfire with branches they had found outside, which triggered the sprinklers. A group of eighth graders led by Chad Middlebrow were encouraging another boy to rub icy hot on his penis.

The whole school had eaten our mushrooms. Ben ran up to me and frantically asked if I was going to help. I didn't respond. All I could do was watch in awe as the chaos unfolded. After a moment, I strolled down the hall toward my room to find the evidence I needed. I passed a group of theater students in a circle singing an almost unrecognizable version of Phantom of the Opera while sprinkler water drizzled down on them. I got to my door and confirmed that the Ziploc bags were empty. It had to have been Julien and Darius.

I took my time packing the belongings I wanted to keep from my desk: an old science fair pin from college, a book with frayed edges that described the human-like behavior of animals, and a few holiday cards the kids had given me. I returned to the commons and pulled up a chair to watch. Then, I heard a voice on the loudspeaker.

"Hello, Elmwood Middle School." The voice said, hesitant but excited. It was Emily from my class. I could hear a giggle behind her.

"We're here with the afternoon announcements," the other voice said, obviously waiting for Emily to take over. It was Jamie.

It was them. I shook my head in disbelief.

Emily jumped back on. "We locked the door to the office, so while Principal Thornbloom is having an aneurysm trying to find the key, we have something we want to say." The loudspeaker gave off the high-pitched squeal that happens when you hold the microphone too close to the receiver, and the students wandering the halls looked up.

"Our teacher, Mr. Brooks, he's not a bad guy." Emily started.

"Not bad at all," Jamie chimed in, the Ed McMahon to Emily's Johnny Carson.

"Earlier this year, someone hurt him. Then he started coming into class tired, like he didn't care anymore. You can tell when a teacher doesn't care — it's kind of sad, right Jamie?"

"Oh yeah, like all the time."

"Right, he stopped teaching from our textbook, and we started this experiment."

I hung my head, expecting to hear next how irresponsible I was — how no real teacher would have his class produce drugs and how much material they had missed as a result. Emily paused her speech for a moment to let me think about it.

"It was awesome. We learned so much."

I perked my head up and smiled wide with pride as the sprinkler water rained down on me.

"So much," Jamie added.

"But mostly, what we learned was how little school teaches you about things that matter a lot. Like, let's say you have a best friend. Don't worry, Jamie, I'm not talking about you."

"Oh good, haha."

"Let's say you have this best friend. You've known her all your life. You've slept over at her house, played soccer together, talked about boys, all that stuff. Then, one day, you overhear her insulting you to some other, cooler friends. She said you were lame and that she wouldn't even let you borrow her shirt if you were freezing. This is when you go into the vortex…"

I couldn't believe I was hearing this. These girls didn't even want to miss class to go to the bathroom. It felt like she was talking only to me, although I could feel other teachers around me listening. Frank banged on the door in the background, trying to get them to stop.

"You go into a vortex where you can't see. You can't see that sometimes bad things can be good because you're just so mad and sad. But they can. Because you aren't hanging out with your friend anymore, you learn to play the guitar, and it becomes your lifelong passion. You find something you couldn't imagine living without. All because your friend insulted you. That's what's going to happen to you, Mr. Brooks — you'll turn that old dirty ground into a great new life, like our mushrooms."

"That's what we're saying," Jamie said, a bit confused at Emily's point.

"When did anyone learn any of that from algebra? Oh, here comes Mr. Thornbloom. He finally found the key." The girls' voices trailed off.

I was almost in tears. I stood up, looked around, and saw the school was still in chaos. Julien rode by me on a skateboard in his underwear and yelled, "I didn't do this, Mr. Brooks." Giggles and loud belly laughs were everywhere.

I walked out to the front of the school and looked up at the overcast spring day. The girls were right: reinvention is our superpower; I should put it to use. I slung my backpack over my shoulder, like a student coming from his last day, and began walking home. I wanted the time to think, explore, and give myself permission to dream up something different for my life since I no longer had a job, a partner, or a place to live.

Stephen Elmer

A dish best served cold

Dear Diary, isn't that the way I should start? Who knows, I'm no Bridget Jones, I'm just me — Marie. Marie Grey. Ring any bells? I don't suppose so. I'm that insignificant person in the corner, the pallid nobody, the ghost-chef of the Pimlico laboratory. If you followed me scurrying down Piccadilly to my grimy bedsit you might wonder at my curious farmyard odour, sharp with the metallic zest of blood, but that's what happens when you spend your days sifting through offal for the next big food fetish. The fact that I'm the restaurant's top ideas man — or, in my case, woman — doesn't seem to factor anywhere.

Pick a paper, any paper and there you'll see him, my boss, Gaston — bold as horseradish, subtle as chorizo, his trademark glasses reeking with self-importance. You can't fail to notice his enormous forehead, glossy with the grease of false pride; a third or fourth wife cackling on his arm as they count his multimillions. And doctorates? He's got a brace of cooked-up honorary Doctorates in Science from some godforsaken Home Counties poly-tec-turned-uni; a Chemistry fellowship; a gong from the Queen and his own ridiculous coat of arms featuring a fat boar with basil Gules and a poor impression of the what-will-become-infamous *sashimi bōchō* knife that he brandishes whenever a member of the paparazzi glides into orbit.

And his house? Have you seen the inside of his poxy townhouse? I'm sure it's been featured in *Tasteless Country Vogue* or *Crap Home Ideas* magazine. He probably didn't waltz the journo up to his ego-attic den though, where the walls are papered with an award for this, a lifetime achievement for that, photos from *GQ* magazine, not to mention BAFTA nominations and book covers. It's sickening, utterly sickening, especially when you know that his fame rests on the blade-edge of my fertile imagination. I'm the one with the real Chemistry degree, the Bachelor's in Culinary Arts and the fantastical ingenuity.

So who am I? Well, Marie as I said. OK, I'll even allow insignificant as I stand only five feet tall in my clumpy chef's clogs. Quiet (he calls me Mary Mouse sometimes, twat), unassuming but actually quite, quite brilliant. I'm pretty sure you've worked out what I do by now. So, on my *resumé*.... seaslug granita. You've heard of it? Well, that was me. Frogs legs crystals on a *yuzu* lily leaf? Beef brains with a Wagyu foam? Red ant egg soup with a dash of *ponzu*? *Muktuk* licorice allsorts? Chocolate weevil mash? Everything that includes liquid nitrogen? Me, all me. You've probably seen him gurning over a conical Erlenmeyer flask or his safety-goggled eyes reflected in the glassy dazzle of some wildly expensive distillation apparatus. But ask him how to use a pycnometer or whether to use calcium or sodium chloride in food spherification and I think you'll find him looking over his shoulder for me:

"I fink you'd find it easier to understand," patronising in his cod-French accent, "if eet was put in simple layman's terms by my lab girl, little Marie 'ere ." Insincere grin.

"So why am I still there?" I hear you ask. At 'The Purple Boar' in deepest Berkshire? Someone with my qualifications could easily move to a restaurant where I would be properly appreciated. Well, apart from the fact that 'Il Trulli', the only other place I really wanted to work, has finally closed its

Apulian doors, I've been happy enough. I've been biding my time, honing my art, travelling round the world picking up new techniques, discovering new ingredients, playing food-Goddess in the nirvana of my kitchen. And waiting for the overdue moment that he would put me in charge of one of his offshoot restaurants, 'The Piggery' perhaps or 'Trough'.

But seriously just right now, I have bloody had enough. The man has gone one step too far. And in the national press too, not just the petty *Berks Gazette*. I don't care if his poncey 'Boar' does need a publicity boost. So what if he lost hundreds of bookings when the discovery of a spiteful intestinal parasite shut us down briefly this summer? In my so very humble opinion, he should be herding them back through the doors by gastronomy not garrulous preaching.

However, this week on national tv:

"Women can't make it to the top in cooking because they can't 'andle the pressure. Then there's their 'ormones, their body clock. Every month I 'ave to tip-toe around my female staff [that's me I guess] and I can't even mention their attitude wivvout them stalking into the cold room in a snit. Then, sooner or later, they want to settle down and 'ave kids. You can't be a dedicated cook and 'ave kids. Top chefs can't 'ave children and succeed."

Oh really, my friend?

You do.

Ah yes of course! One of your fragrant wives stays at home to cosset the kids. But guess what...I have a wife too.

"And then there's the 'eavy pans."

In the gospel according to St Gaston, us delicate types don't have the sheer muscle power to become the top cow in the canteen. Well, firstly, I can lift a heavy dish with the best of them (and, by the way, there's many a dainty male chef who needs a pantry HeMan to help heave the stock pot). And secondly: who needs to lift a sodding *bain-marie* the size of the QE 2 if you have genius brains peppered with a dose of sly kitchen cunning.

I already have my plan in place to become the top sow in this pigpen. It's a dish best served icy cold and requires no lifting whatsoever. Well, maybe just one small lift and that was the EU ban on the poisonous Japanese blowfish, *fugu*. A ban that shackled our tasting menu when the 'Boar's' diners were calling out for ever-more sensational experiences. And to be fair, you can't get more exciting than dicing with death: just a sliver of fugu liver can turn you into a zombie. No kidding — within an hour you're not even a dead man walking, you're just dead. Skin, gonads and liver from a single blowfish can kill 30 people. What a fish!

Now we're out of the EU and Brexit-free to make our own rules, I have invented a new dish that will blow Gazza's mind. Literally. Icy shards of piggy pink *fugu sashimi* under a ponzu cloud and, because the fugu has almost no flavour, I will garnish it with the thinnest rashers of incendiary Black Spanish radish and a filigree made from *mirin* and essence of fiercely pungent Norwegian *lutefisk*. I picture it served in *sarcocypha austriaca*, scarlet elf cup, a wild fungi I can source from the ramson wood near my parent's house where I forage the leaves for my aromatic wild garlic and chocolate ganache raviolo. He will almost certainly want to add some elaborate table piece with a teeny automaton wearing a *yukata* and playing a tiny, probably tinny, Japanese *shaminsen*.

I have no doubt that Gaston will be able to source fresh blowfish from his friend Akemi Shaguhachi who runs 'Shokudu' in Knightsbridge. And me? I will source the killer ingredients from my friend Hibachi in Kamakura, the small Japanese seaside resort I visited in 2016. Lovely Hib owes me since I helped him become a billi-yen-aire with some extraordinarily innovative recipes for his start-up café. And I know he's not above some scullery skulduggery — how do you think he got the café in the first place?

It will need some sleight of hand for me to slip my toxic tickles into the blowfish slices that Gaston will have insisted on filleting himself — how else could he claim the fame for the newest and wildest ingredient to hit our shores? But I can't see this as too difficult for a little Mouse like me, especially a Mouse who just may have had a practice run with contaminated water back in June when the giardia crisis occurred!

Before the end of service, the effects of the tetrodotoxin will be whirling through the restaurant like a tornado in Kansas: paralysed diners will be tumbling off their chairs, their Armani suits and Beckham frocks frowsty with the fetid bouquet of sweat and rancid stench of vomit. Speechless in their living-dead-despair, they won't even be able to scream. And I will sit patiently while they suffocate to death, comforting a distraught Gaston while we wait for the police and the manslaughter charges that will surely lead him all the way to jail. It's a little bit of collateral damage, but hey, nothing ventured, nothing gained!

In the Shimonoseki region, famous for its blowfish, they pronounce fugu as 'fuku'. According to my friend Hibachi, fuku sounds like 'good fortune' in Japanese. But to me it sounds like Gaz's luck will have packed its bags and headed for the hills. And all I can say to that is: Gaston — well, I don't even have to say it, do I?

❀

'The Purple Mouse', Cricket Lane, Grave RG6 6SZ (0324 78623)

Halloween tasting menu for two: £300. Wine flight: £120 each.

Review: Kay Drizzlar

'The Monster Mash' by Bobby 'Boris' Pickett and the Crypt Kickers shook the rafters of this tiny boutique restaurant deep in the Berkshire darkness as we entered. It was an entirely appropriate welcome to the Halloween Special Tasting Menu on offer from the kitchen of chef patron Marie Grey. You, my regular readers, will know that I utterly despise a tasting menu but the chance to witness the launch of 'The Purple Mouse' (previously 'The Purple Boar') after the tragic catastrophe sixteen months ago that saw original chef George Brown (aka Gaston St. Sanglier) up in court for involuntary manslaughter, was an opportunity too good to miss.

It had been long suspected by the 'Boar's' intrepid diners, and those in the know, that the inspiration for the extraordinary culinary masterpieces that Sanglier brought to the table with his special brand of 'gallic' je ne sais quoi, were devised by his associate Marie although she was never publicly acknowledged as the brains behind his brawn. Menu highlights such as dancing shrimps served live in a sauce of locally sourced herbs (a street food rarely found inside a restaurant even in its native region of north east Thailand) had initially established the original restaurant's bizarre though very fine reputation before it was beset by a duo of disasters starting with the so-called Giardia Crisis and ending with the death of five diners by a lethal chemical called tetrodotoxin found in the liver of the puffer fish. So, it was with my heart in my mouth that I pulled on my best bib and tucker, tucked my courage into my Doc Marten's and made my way to Grave to see if Marie would be able to rise to this festive occasion.

The service was attentive without being overbearing. Staff on this spooky night were dressed as vampires, capes and incisors flashing in the dim lighting, though I was assured upon on asking that their normal costume was an elegant grey. Indeed, the whole restaurant is elegantly grey (can this be a pun on Marie's surname?) with table linens and drapes in 50 shades of purple and tiny lilac mice on the serviettes. It's a little twee but I got it — anything to get away from the macho décor of the 'Boar' days.

The coffin-shaped menu was not so much a list of dishes but rather a dictionary of astonishing ingredients — some of which (and I know you may find this hard to believe) were new even to me. There was indeed a monster mash — a sumac-y soupçon topped with the crunch of Colombian fat bottomed ants — and, as befits Halloween, there were plenty of body parts: tuna eyeballs, a pickled slice of skin and blubber from a narwhal here, a sliver of jellied moose nose there, a dash of squid intestines fermented in their own viscera served with a tot of snake blood liquor. But this was a menu of tiny dishes which, I regret to say, revolted rather than delighted and I haven't even begun to mention an apparent preoccupation with insects such as digger wasps, silkworm pupae and snout beetle larvae. It's fair to say that by course number six I would have given my own eye teeth for a ramekin of something as bland as shepherd's pie.

Marie Grey, if indeed it was her who designed the often surreal but always delicious dishes for 'The Purple Boar', appears to have lost her mojo mired as it must surely be, deep within the bloody carcasses of animals that should never be called on to grace a Berkshire table. And all served, if I may say so, without the outrageous aplomb of her previous boss. I cannot imagine that this current resurrection of a restaurant on Cricket Lane will last even half as long as Sanglier's two-year suspended sentence.

Dear readers, look elsewhere for your outlandish foodie fix, for this is not the case of the mouse that roared.

Siobhan Gifford

You can go away

I want to tell you about a man who died ten years ago. Thomas Russell.

He'd recently moved into Beckside House, a rather expensive residential home in my parish. There weren't many men in there, but it was the women who were uncomfortable with a 'lady vicar'. Still, they mostly got over that, and several came to my monthly communion service. A few people confided in me. Thomas did, eventually.

Our first encounter was in Beckside's comfortable 'Rose Lounge'. Spritely old women were admiring a gurgling baby, someone's newest great-grandchild, held up by a proud young mother for their adoration. I heard a hoarse muttering near me: "None of that lovey-dovey stuff for me. Left me in the pram, down the garden, all day long, that's what my mother told me she did." Turning, I saw a man who looked so sad that I put out a comforting hand; he flinched away. The women ignored him.

Thomas wasn't easy to talk to because his hearing was almost gone, damaged during a lifetime of working on noisy sites with heavy machinery. However, I could listen. He was a civil engineer, a practical man, and he once said to me: "I never understood people, I know that. But things — structures, materials, solid objects — I thought I understood how they worked. Seems I didn't even get that right."

I've pieced his story together.

Thomas married in his twenties, and stayed married until the day between Christmas and New Year when he watched the monitor attached to his wife, Esther, flatline. He came home from the hospital and knew immediately he could not stay in their house. Seeing her shoes waiting mutely in the hall told him that. He pushed them into a corner.

After her cremation, in a room full of people he did not recognise who told him Esther was 'so strong' and 'wonderful', he was advised more than once that he shouldn't make important decisions until he'd 'got over it'. His son Matthew came from New Zealand for a week and said the same thing. Thomas didn't tell Matthew that he'd heard that before, forty years before, and it hadn't helped then.

When someone dies, there's a lot to do. It is only after the funeral, after the visitors have gone home, that people start to realise what has happened. Alone in the house, Thomas couldn't sleep. When he lay down and closed his eyes he would hear a child's hungry wail and then Esther's gentle murmurs to the baby — often, but not always, Matthew — nuzzling at her breast. He saw Matthew wave goodbye across an airport barrier and turn his back. He heard Esther: "You're not trapped like me." Sometimes the sobs that woke him were his own.

Thomas and Esther had lived in the same house throughout their marriage. Esther was always a stay-at-home wife, devoting herself to their children and later throwing herself into good causes. She helped with Guides, volunteered at the hospital, served in a hospice shop. Thomas felt excluded from her life: "She didn't want me. She used to say, 'I've spent all day being busy; I just want to watch television.' Then she'd sit knitting blanket squares, glued to Coronation Street. Of course, that was after Matthew'd left home, much later."

Esther ran all their domestic affairs. Absorbed in his job and professionally successful, Thomas often worked away, including abroad. When he reached 65 and retired in the early 1990s, he realised that she used their house mainly as a base for her outside activities, piling leaflets and papers everywhere. She served him dull meals on unmatched crockery. Only when she was diagnosed with a cancer that rapidly spread into her bones and she spent long days at home, did her surroundings irritate her. By then it was too late for changes. She hadn't enough energy to let Thomas do so much as paint the walls. "It's all right for you. You're not trapped like me. You can go away." As she grew weaker her voice became quieter, but he heard everything she said. Even when it was unspoken.

At the beginning of her illness, Esther told him she didn't need him; then, when she admitted she did, he couldn't help her. He no longer recognised the jolly, bossy Sunday-School-piano-playing girl he had married, or the plumply pregnant mother of his children who had ideas about curtains and carpets, or the self-contained busybody who neglected their home but joined committees and societies and campaigns.

Thomas would have liked to spend some of their last weeks together reminiscing or looking through old albums, but Esther did not want to and he did not know how to persuade her. He came home from shopping one day to see patches on the walls where their family photographs had hung. Esther had found the strength to destroy them all, breaking frames, tearing cardboard. She would do nothing, either for herself or for Thomas, to soften her dying. She would go alone into the darkness. She refused to speak to Matthew when he rang.

Two days before she died, Thomas went upstairs and found her bed empty. She was not in the bathroom, not in the kitchen, but outside by the dustbin, wearing only a nightgown, and with her thin bare feet thrust into her old brown shoes. He told me she was saying, "I waited and waited for you," but that she stared past him and through him. He helped her back to bed, then went outside and looked in the bin. Among the rubbish he found the tiny child's sandal Esther had kept under her pillow for years. Grateful that it at least had survived, he wiped it and locked it safely inside his briefcase.

And when she had gone, leaving him in a bleakly empty house, the need for untroubled sleep gave Thomas an idea. He bought an old VW campervan and discovered he slept well in it, so he stayed away for two or three nights at a time, then a week. It became harder and harder to return. He took out a mobile phone contract. He didn't explain to Matthew why he no longer used his landline. In the end he put his house into the hands of estate agents, asking them to call in a clearance firm to get rid of everything. He packed a couple of suitcases, pushed the photograph albums Esther had refused to look at into his briefcase, gave a few mementos to people who'd known her, then — not knowing what else to do with it — he put the urn containing Esther's ashes into a locker in the van. As he looked back into the hall for the last time, he spotted her shoes, almost out of sight in the corner.

Cool and stiff in his hands, they retained the shape of her small broad feet; he heard the sound of her brisk step as she went out in the morning, and then the slow shuffle that had replaced it at the end of her life. Moved by an impulse he did not understand, he stowed them under the passenger seat before opening the road atlas, turning to the index and wondering at English place-names: Amwell, Redruth, Shoeburyness...

That first night, in a car park somewhere in the Midlands, Esther came to him again. "It's all right for you. You can go away." Nevertheless, he slept soundly until he was woken by the weeping of a child, very young and very frightened. Outside the van, nothing moved under the dismal yellow sodium lighting. He rolled down a window to work out where the crying was coming from, but all he could hear was the monotonous hum of traffic and the sudden yowling of a cat. A cold wind rattled bits of rubbish at the roadside. It was just before dawn when Thomas rolled up his sleeping bag and started the engine. Esther's shoes had slid forward and their toes peeped from under the seat; roughly, he shoved them back.

One day in March he got lost in the suburban streets of a northern town. Looking for a turning place, he drove past a pub into a cul-de-sac and saw a 'For Sale' sign outside a dilapidated house half-hidden in an overgrown garden. The sun was setting. Thomas pulled into the driveway, parked behind a large tree and decided to stay there overnight. He opened his briefcase and took out his wallet, checking he had enough money to go to the pub.

After steak pie and three pints of beer he again slept soundly. Esther came to him, telling him, "It's all right for you. You can go away," and a baby cried, but he felt soothed rather than upset. In the morning he saw the photograph albums, his wallet and the little shoe on top of his briefcase; he resolved to be more careful about putting things away.

Thomas explored the area and made enquiries. A practical man, as I said, he needed a project: he negotiated a lower purchase price for the property. He had the van so it didn't matter that the building was uninhabitable. He worked on the house and garden, becoming a familiar figure in building suppliers' yards and garden centres. Neighbours took an interest, sometimes stopping to chat, sometimes helping, and occasionally women would bring him a cake or a casserole. Did I say he had tinnitus as well as hearing loss? Still, when the noises in his head were quiet, Thomas was happy.

Sometimes though, on bad days, he had to listen hard to establish that the sounds he heard — chatter and laughter, televisions, piano practice, drums being thumped in garages, children squabbling — were real. And every now and then there was Esther's voice. "It's all right for you. You're not trapped." Sometimes, particularly at dawn and dusk, the sounds he heard were those of a woman calling or a child crying, and then he would look for some noisily practical task or go to the pub with its comfortable clatter of glasses and hiss of beer taps.

However, one warm summer evening, the child's crying and the woman's calling were so persistent he felt compelled to investigate. Searching for the voices, he came to a tumble-down wall with a shallow stream on its far side. His heart thumped as he saw a very young child, a little girl, sprawled in the water, her leg somehow caught by a branch. He scrambled over the wall, freed her leg and picked her up. Supporting her under her armpits, holding her away from him, he carried her in front of him almost like a sacrificial offering. A tall dark-haired woman with tears streaming down her face ran towards them. "Oh, thank you! Lucy, whatever happened? You naughty girl!" Thomas left them there, the child with her arms round her mother's neck and her mother's arms hugging her close, both of them laughing and crying. Arriving home, glancing into the campervan as he passed it, he saw Esther's old shoes had slid forward, and the little sandal was on the passenger seat. He didn't remember opening his briefcase.

It's a cliché that news travels fast, but that weekend the local paper's headline read: 'Mother praises campervan hero'. More people spoke to him, in and out of the pub. He learned whose brother-in-law's mini-digger would sort out the garden, which carpet shops had good fitters... The work was finished just before the clocks went back, and the pub landlord suggested a house-warming party, volunteering to cater for it. Thomas invited drinking acquaintances, neighbours, people who had helped him, Lucy and her mother, and even the reporter from the Enquirer. At last he felt he belonged.

It was a good party. "Thinking of selling your old van, Tom?" one of his guests, a second-hand car dealer, asked. "I've got a customer looking for one. There's a really nice Golf on the forecourt that I reckon would suit you." They shook hands on a deal, and as he locked the door before going up to bed Thomas told himself he would empty and clean the van in the morning. The novelty of popularity, and lying between proper sheets in a room with carpet and curtains, kept him awake for a while. He took out the photograph albums from his briefcase and looked through them before he slept.

Clearing out the van, he rediscovered the urn at the back of the locker. No nearer knowing what to do with it, or with Esther's old shoes, he put them carefully into the cupboard under the stairs. That night he was visited by Esther and

Amy, and between them they made him relive the terrible events of forty years ago. In the morning, exhausted and shaking, he tripped over the tiny sandal he thought he had stowed carefully in a briefcase pocket. The cupboard door was open and he saw the urn had fallen from its shelf, while ashes speckled the shoes he had placed on the floor.

In his tidy overheated room at Beckside House, with its faint smell of disinfectant and air freshener, he told me what had happened: "She wasn't quite two when we lost her. Amy. I was at work, Esther was at home. Amy liked to potter in and out through the French windows into the garden. Maybe Esther dozed off. Three months pregnant. She got tired in the afternoons. Anyway, she called Amy, who didn't come. She looked in the garden — couldn't find her. She looked everywhere in the house, then in the garden again. There was a red Clark's sandal near a narrow gap in the hedge. Hardly a hundred millimetres. One of Amy's first 'big girl' shoes. We didn't have a phone. Esther didn't dare go far from the house in case she suddenly reappeared. Amy. By the time I came home, she was desperate. White face. Red eyes. I went to the phone box and dialled 999 and knocked on the doors of people further down the street. It was getting dark. Those days — I can't remember them very well. Esther cried and called, and called and cried. They dragged the river. People looked in their coal cellars. She used to wake me up, Esther, every night. 'Amy's out there. I know she is. Can't you hear her crying?' I'd listen, but I could hear nothing. I'd look about outside — no sign of Amy. Nothing. Never. I had to go back to work. What else could I do? She thought I didn't care."

I was still wondering how to react when he resumed: "I wanted to move, but people told us not to make important decisions until we'd 'got over it'. Esther refused. What if Amy came home and we weren't there? When Matthew was born, she said: 'We must never let him know we lost his sister. He won't trust us. We won't talk about her.' That was that.

"Three bedrooms, we had. Curtains and carpet she'd chosen for Amy, she made me get them out. I painted over her pink wallpaper. I had to sleep in there — she couldn't even open the door. Our old bedroom — well, she moved the cot in. New curtains, new carpet. She shared that room with Matthew till long after he'd started school. She liked him with her, in the bed. He had to ask and ask to get his own room.

"All the photographs of Amy had to be taken down. I put them in an album. Esther wouldn't open it. Mind you, as a baby Matthew looked just like her. Amy. She kept that sandal under her pillow and held it in her hand when Matthew was asleep. She was trying to be ready for Amy, and to stop Matthew ever knowing he'd had a sister and we'd lost her. She couldn't let him out of her sight. I couldn't bear it. I went away a lot for work, sometimes overseas.

"I just wasn't needed. When Matthew went to school, she walked him there, collected him at dinner-time, took him back and then was at the gates again. She did housework and shopping, then filled her day up with voluntary work. After he'd moved into his own bedroom, she kept her room door open, so she'd know if he even turned over in his sleep. Matthew was a clever boy; he did well. When he grew up, he wanted to spread his wings. I don't blame him. Esther got more and more involved with her organisations, especially those dealing with children, until she was worn out. He left home. He went into the travel industry, and now he's settled in New Zealand. He couldn't have gone further away from us."

We sat in silence for a while, and then he spoke again. "I've put Esther's shoes over there, and Amy's sandal in between them. I don't know how else to help them find each other." Thomas's face was shiny with tears and his hand shook as he gestured towards the footwear he had kept for so long. I looked where he pointed, and saw a very small faded red sandal tucked protectively between cracked old brown shoes.

"I've still got the urn, too. I don't know what Esther wants me to do, Vicar. She comes here, and I hear her: 'It's all right for you. You're not trapped like me. You can go away.' But I can't. She went into the darkness alone. She wouldn't take any comfort. When I follow her, will I be like her? Will she still be calling for Amy, and Amy crying for her?"

I have thought about Thomas a lot since he died. I wish I could have helped him to receive the Holy Spirit, the Comforter. But I didn't, and I don't know the answers to his questions. He never thought that Esther and Amy might have been calling for him.

He doesn't go away. Thomas Russell haunts me.

Susan Perkins

Humming birds among the runner beans

She puts away the wax crayons, the thick paper,
rolls up the imprint of those pious downcast eyes,
folded hands, demure small feet, the memorial
she rubbed so hard the paper tore.

Despite the cold stone under her knees, she has found
peace in this lonely church, shadowed by ancient yews
and something of acceptance. This will be the last time,
the last of the last times. She closes the door behind her,
ready to walk into her new life.

What do you do when you find your brand new house, put your brand new key in the brand new lock, push open a door onto disaster? Ladders, plaster dust, timber. The steep pitched roof is on, walls and window frames. The furniture vans arrive tomorrow. Jennie's awake and miserable as only a tired 6-year-old can be, Robbie's asleep in his car seat. We are cold, tired and hungry after an 8-hour flight from London, and a 5-hour journey up-country from Halifax. It is dusk and starting to snow, and I am just about holding it together. If this is what emigrating to Canada entails, my hard won optimism is a tea-light in a gale force wind.

There are very few times when I've had to make a choice. Usually if I wait long enough, I get pushed in one direction or the other by a shove in my back, or a tug on my arm. I've always lived by the maxim you regret what you didn't do, not the things you did. You find a way to make it work, even if it was a mistake. This time there was no-one to push or drag me down one path instead of another. Did I agree to emigrate or not, it was as simple as that, and as difficult. Clamouring voices said we'd regret it, or we'd just love the challenge. In the end I agreed we'd go.

So here we are. John is stoical and practical. He'd been out 6 months earlier to tie up the details of his appointment at the hospital and to design a house on the plot of land we had bought in a new development nearby. He'd had the foresight to build into the contract with the builder that if the house wasn't ready, we'd be put up at their expense in the motel down the road. So that was where we go next, four of us in what amounts to a beach chalet in a pulp and paper town in Eastern Canada surrounded by spruce forests.

Next day the removal truck unloads our precious little bit of England into an empty basement. Houses in New Brunswick are built half underground, sensible in a place where snow comes in November and stays till May, dumping 260 inches. By the end of the winter the snow banks each side of our drive will be well over my head. The windows of the basement rooms are at ground level, so the rooms are warm in winter and cool in the hot humid summers. Our furniture sits down there for weeks, and a night watchman dozes on a dust-sheeted settee protecting it all.

We move in at last. Upstairs is a lovely light and airy open-plan living space. Big windows look out on a fairyland of spruce and birch, glittering with snow. A sparkling white carpet lies round the house. John goes to work, the children and I get mumps, and my life narrows to bedroom and bathroom. My face balloons too, and when my ears and my shoulders made a gentle curve, I get into bed with them. We are 3 chipmunks, hibernating. I have never felt so miserable.

As winter gets into its stride, we learn to listen to the local news station when we get up. If there is danger of freezing flesh, the school will be closed and we won't walk down the road to wait for the school bus. We make a deal with a local contractor to clear our driveway after a heavy blizzard. We wake in the night to the low growl of the snowblower and know that the blizzard had gone and we will be able to get out in the morning.

We get used to plugging the car into a heating unit in the carport overnight and using one at the supermarket if the temperature is below -20C. We wear padded boots, snowsuits, and thick gloves. We ski, toboggan and learn to skate. We have barbecues in snowbound forest clearings, and day after day the sun shines in a cloudless blue sky. We love it.

You can have too much of a good thing. After 4 months I long for soft rain, mist and something green. Then in April someone out there flicks a switch, and the temperature rises. The sun is hot and the snow begins to melt. Each morning another layer dissolves around the house. Soggy half eaten sandwiches appear, broken tiles, plasterboard, wood, all the debris from a hastily finished house. Each morning I waddle on my snowshoes like a foraging duck pecking at the scattered remains. Each day another feast is spread out for me to sample. Finally in May only a few mounds of snow lie under the trees, but our lovely white carpet is now a sea of mud.

I put on my English gumboots, and while the children are in school, I spread topsoil, plant grass seed, make flower beds and plan a vegetable patch. The long skiing holiday is over, I begin to feel I can put down a few roots. Maybe I can grow here. I still think sometimes of the quiet country churches, where I did the brass rubbings that we brought with us. I write home every week.

The roots hold. The lawn greens, roses bloom. Tomatoes, squash, and sweetcorn grow with tropical speed. We make friends, go to parties at the beach, and when it gets too hot retreat to the half-finished basement where I read to the children and we live through all the *Little House on the Prairie* books, only coming back to the present for meals. We buy a puppy, and if I am lonely, I find things to do. I volunteer at the school. Ricky and Dicky are identical twins I can never tell apart who love to mix me up when we practice reading. Another little boy, Pete really struggles in class but loves to draw, so he draws things he likes and I write the names underneath. The first word he learns is 'bombardier', a small snow blowing machine. Don't we both feel great! I do a Literacy for Adults course and wonder what happened to the gentle shy man who came to learn to read and did so well. I buy a kiln and a wheel and set up a little pottery in the basement.

The summer is hot and sunny day after day. I long for the drizzle and mists of Devon and a walk on the moor. My roots are thirsty!

Heat blowtorched the lawn,
sucked the scent from roses,
blushed tomatoes overnight
and blew up pumpkins like balloons.

It swelled the sweetcorn teets
and hung a scarlet net for humming birds

to swim like fish among the runner beans.

The summer simmered,
stirred a feast
served up so hot
it burnt a tongue
that longed for veils of summer rain
and dripping leaves.

The small plane circles low over the house twice, then flies west into the setting sun. We race out of the house and get in the car. We follow it, trying to avoid the potholes, the children bouncing in the back, chanting 'faster, Mummy, faster.' The road is empty, thank goodness, or I'd be a liability. The airfield is a stretch of level ground a mile away. The little plane waits quietly, having chased off the chipmunks and scared away the birds. Standing in the shade under the wing is a tall young man, bending to talk to a slim grey-haired lady who hardly comes up to his shoulder. She sees us, crouches down and opens her arms. The children tear across the field, throw themselves at her, and all three collapse on the ground laughing. The pilot is Joe, a good friend of ours who is clocking up air-miles to get his commercial pilot's licence; his only passenger is my mother coming from England to spend the summer with us.

Driving back to the house with us, she tells us how much safer she'd felt sitting beside Joe and feeding him polo mints, sweets he calls candies and says he's never had before; how he'd pointed out all sorts of interesting things below them, as they followed the highway from Halifax, Nova Scotia, to Bathurst, New Brunswick, for 300 miles, dead straight most of the way; how he'd come straight up to her in the arrivals hall, recognised her so easily from our description; how they'd walked across the tarmac to his two-seater Cessna and waited in line between the jumbo jets for their turn to take off; how she'd heard the roar of the jumbo behind them chasing them into the sky. She tells us what a lovely young man Joe is, and how pleased she is that he'll be taking her back to Halifax at the end of her stay, they've got to know each other so well.

Summer comes in without knocking here, Spring gets elbowed out when the temperature soars from freezing to tropical almost overnight. Granny left England in warm gentle rain. It is in the 90's here and the sun blazes in a technicolour sky. We retreat to the cool basement rooms and she settles down on the old settle we brought from England with us. A child snuggles up on each side of her and she tells Ben and Fred stories. Ben and Fred are two little boys their age, who are best friends. Some stories are about brave kind little boys, some stories are about naughty little boys. They get to choose which story line they want.

The days are uneventful, full of made-up stories, games, Scot Joplin playing in the background, three generations sharing the summer. The days slide by slowly at first but quicken as the harvest ripens, the days cool. The last week seems to evaporate like morning mist.

Granny packs her case, puts the cards and pictures from the children flat on the bottom, and we drive to the airfield. Joe is waiting, we all hug and hug again, Granny gets in, the engine roars, she waves from the window, the plane taxies, lifts, flies off like small bird. We stand and wave till it is out of sight. Then John and I swing the children between us and talk about how much they will have to tell Granny next time they see her. We get in the car and go home. The children stare out of the window, not speaking.

After they are in bed, I go into her bedroom to change the sheets, sit on the bed and wait till the echo of her voice fades away.

✳

Our introduction to summer entertaining is a big party with our neighbours, the Petries, who have at least 6 if not 7 children, and love parties. We have washing up bowls full of lobsters, lots of bread, lots of beer and wine, and lots of stories and jokes. Their son Peter will become the children's favourite babysitter. We will see a lot of the warm hearted and generous Petries.

We are making some good friends. Ralph and Helen have taken us under their wing. They have a beach house on the shore, and we have long lazy summer afternoons sitting on the deck watching Jennie and Robbie playing on the beach with their son Danny. He is a gentle soul, a young man who is taking longer to grow up than most, and will probably always need help with the complications of life. The children love him, he is on their wavelength. We have celebratory meals with Ralph and Helen for birthdays and anniversaries, and they help to fill the gap left by our own parents. They worry about how Danny will cope when they are gone. None of us could see then that 30 years on it will be Danny who is taking care of Helen, widowed and living in Nova Scotia. When we have lobster, which is cheap here, Helen is the one who loves the dark meat in the head, the bit I can't cope with. Helen's the one who remembers birthdays, and anniversaries. Helen's the one who will reach across the years and the miles and continue to keep in touch when she is a frail lady in her nineties.

Our other honorary grandparents are Frank and Eileen. They live out of town as Frank works at the zinc smelter — the largest smelter in Canada and a major employer in the town. Their children are grown up and living away, so they sometimes have Jennie and Robbie for a sleepover at the weekend. Frank and Robbie do important jobs outside, while Eileen knits trousers and jackets for Jennie's teddy bear and they do 'cooking' together.

Marianne is another good friend. She is Swiss, and in charge of nursing staff at the hospital. She keeps bees, has geese and a goat, loves gardening, picking wild strawberries and making jam. She takes t-bone steaks back to Switzerland at Christmas for her relatives. When she comes back to Canada after the holiday she heaves a sigh of relief; it is so good to be able to flush the loo after 10 pm or play the radio, have a party and not worry about the noise. Apartment living just isn't her thing. She is the one person who understands why I love to go for a solitary walk in the rain.

Michel and Karen are outdoor folk too. We go cross-country skiing with them, and come home for cinnamon toast by the fire. Michel takes Robbie fishing for flounder in the bay. They come back laden with fish. Robbie believes all you have to do is drop in your line and the fish queue up to be caught. Michel's a good artist and introduces Jennie to painting with an easel and palette. He has endless patience with the children. One day he'll be a great father.

Sue and Mike often come skiing too, or for picnics in the summer, the six of us, plus the children are very comfortable together. Mike is from Poland, Michel and Karen from Belgium, Sue from the far side of Canada. One of the first questions on meeting someone new here is what brings you to Bathurst? It's out in the sticks after all. But we meet lovely people. One of the things about ending up in a small isolated town is that people make the effort to be neighbourly.

John spends one summer in Toronto, studying, and so many people make the effort to see I am not lonely. Some weekends Sue and Mike, Michel and Karen will come round to barbecue, we'll sit on the deck listening to Scott Joplin and playing with the children. Other days we will go to the beach with Ralph and Helen and share their beach house.

The days pass easily, but most nights the children share the bed with me. We're happier that way. Even the dog is allowed in the bedroom, but there is no room on the bed.

I am learning that it is not the place but the people that make it possible to put down roots and thrive. We are making it happen.

❋

Autumn arrives as suddenly as Spring. The switch is flipped again. The colours are spectacular that first year, maples on fire, aspen incandescent, and the harvest overflows. I collect the squash, and the pumpkins. Pulp tomatoes that have flowed like a red tide into the kitchen all summer long. We have breakfasted outside since May watching humming birds swimming in the air as they drank from the scarlet flowers of the runner beans I grew round the deck. Now it is time for the humming birds to leave and to harvest the last of the beans.

The days grow shorter, I sweep up the leaves, put a wire cage around the roses, and fill it with leaves to protect them. The ground will be frozen for the next four months. I hope their roots will have burrowed deep and will hold firm.

I get out our snowsuits and wait for the snow to come. The seasons do not soften into one another like a watercolour landscape. Here vivid colours collide: summer is a fluorescent blue, scarlet and gold; Autumn catches fire; and now everything is dazzling white on white. In May next year I will ache for green, will fall in love with unfurling leaves and fresh grass, but now glittering icicles hanging from the eaves, snow frosting the birch trees, and clean sheeted snow as far as the eye can see is just magical. I love it.

The temperature rarely rises above zero now. An old wooden house burnt to the ground recently. The air is tinder dry. I burned a pile of cardboard boxes, and they went up like a torch, frightening me.

At the beach the sea is frozen near the shore, the children are fascinated, the dog looks for the seagulls, but they have gone inland.

The scarlet thread in the outdoor thermometer shrinks till only the tip shows. We listen to the local radio each morning. If the school is open, I get Jennie and Robbie into their snowsuits, padded boots, hats, gloves and scarves, then put on my snowsuit, padded boots, hat, gloves and scarf. Eventually we are ready to go up the lane for the school bus. It all takes time, but we haven't missed the bus yet.

John leaves for the hospital before us. Once after a really heavy snowfall he skied across the fields, and found he was the only doctor there. He delivered babies that day.

Today it is bright and windless, the children are at school and I take Meg, our red-haired adolescent setter for her morning run on the ski trail. The land here is flat and covered with spruce forest, there are miles of cross-country ski trails through the trees. It is well below freezing this morning but after a while I warm up, take off my down jacket and tie it round my waist. This is my prayer time, my quiet time. The snow blankets all sound, no birds sing in the spruce trees, there's no car or aeroplane noise, no human voices, just the shush of a snow pillow falling from a branch, Meg panting, the hiss of my skis. Neighbours worry that I go out alone, but I have never felt afraid in the woods.

When we get back, I drive to the mall for groceries. It is cold today, the covers over the sewers are sending wisps of warmth smoking into the air. Some folk leave their engines running just in case. I shall be quick. At this time of year, we plug the car into a heater for the engine block overnight, and there are similar plugs in some mall carparks, but not here.

Shopping done I drive home. I'm getting used to driving at half speed on hard packed snow. I am also getting used to shovelling snow from the driveway. The snow banks either side of the drive are already over my head. Our next door neighbour is outside and we wave. She has had her left arm amputated. She can shovel snow as fast as I can, do her own ironing and cycles everywhere in the summer. Whenever I'm tempted to self-pity, I think of her.

I unpack the shopping to the sound of running water. Last week we had no water and the water engineers arrived and unfroze the pipe coming onto the property with an electric current. Now we have to keep a tap open for the rest of the winter, it is like living beside a waterfall. The frost goes down

4 feet, and the pipe wasn't laid deep enough. Because it is all so new to me, I find winter here exciting, but many retired people, the snowbirds, go down to Florida for warmth. Maybe we shall feel that way one day. But for now, we will make the most of the cold and the snow.

It will be a full moon tonight, some friends are coming round and we shall all go tobogganing with the children under the stars. It will be magical, and as light as day.

At the weekend we will have a Weiner roast in the woods. The grown-ups will light a fire on the snow and cook sausages and mull wine, the children will toast marshmallows and build igloos and snowmen and have snowball fights.

Before the snow came we saw the Northern Lights. We woke the children and all climbed onto the roof with sleeping bags. The sky shimmered and pulsed with a silken curtain of every shade of green, blue and silver light. It thundered and throbbed with the silent music of an enormous organ. It was awe inspiring. It is experiences like these that I am storing in a box that I can return to one day far over the horizon.

Up in the attic out of sight
amongst the things I cannot throw away,
I find the holdall with the airline tags,
inside it airmail pages,
tissue thin as trodden autumn leaves,
the weekly letters home
my mother kept for 30 years.

I read and find my voice
tunes to a higher pitch

and interweaves a deeper tone
I recognise but did not hear before,

enmeshed in memories,
I drift between my mother
and my younger self.

I am my mother now
my daughter, me.

The years fall into a pattern, winter is blizzards, snow ploughs, months below freezing, blue skies, wiener roasts in the woods, skis and toboggans. Summer elbows its way in, the snow melts and suddenly it's hot and we retreat to the cool of the basement. Autumn arrives on time, and the sugar maples are a blaze of scarlet, the aspens like spun gold. We grow to love the excitement of the seasons, but I always miss the soft colours of cloudy skies and early morning mist. Six years ago I had to choose, and we have made a good life here, I have been happy. Now there are new decisions to be made, and the choice this time is clearcut: we need to go home.

I have just hugged my husband and strapped my son into the car only half-awake and rubbing the sleep from his eyes. I stand in the driveway waving them out of sight and go back into the house to have my breakfast. There on the breakfast table are their passports and airline tickets Halifax to London, check in time 11pm tonight. It is a long straight road through spruce forest for the next 300 miles, they will see no other cars, maybe a timber truck or two, the sky will lighten, the sun will come up, they won't need to stop till they need gas. No mobile phones in 1982.

I run down the stairs and wake Peter, a medical student who has been staying with us, and has a car, thank God. "Pete, follow that car" It is straight out of a second-rate movie, and as in the movie, he catches up with them 100 miles down the highway. What a star! Back in England I hope he dined out on the story.

Pete goes home. John and Robbie arrive safely in England. Robbie goes to stay with his grandparents, where he will practice eating with a knife as well as a fork, learn to say pavement not sidewalk, rubbish not garbage, and lose his Canadian twang before starting a new school. John will retrieve our old Volvo which has been shipped on ahead, tightly packed with things we will need straight away, and drive down to Truro to start his locum. Months later when we need to change a wheel, we find several 2 litre jars of peanut butter hidden in the wheel arches that we had completely forgotten about.

My grown up 10 year old daughter and I are on our own now. I have finally sold the house. Our time here is shrinking fast as we unpick the threads of the life we have made in the Maritimes. We are going home.

It has been raining all day. So often I have longed for a cloudy day of gentle English rain, but not today. The removal men are soaked to the skin, the container is expertly and tightly packed, and we have just discovered the garden equipment in the shed, and the kiln in my pottery. It feels like a re-run of our arrival in Canada all those years ago, bumping into the unexpected in the dark.

I visit my precious friends, bequeathing the wheelbarrow here, the ladders, spades, and lawnmower there, and crating up the rest to follow us. The container leaves for Halifax, to be shipped to London with all the things we brought out with us 6 years ago.

Jennie and I and Phil, the packer, go downtown to eat and go to a movie. Phil works for G B Liners, the removal firm that had shipped our furniture out from England. Now he has come to stay with us for a week, to pack it all up again. We've made a good team, we've got over the glitches, and now we can celebrate and show him our one-horse town. Phil later wrote a great article for his firm's magazine about his trip. It had been cheaper to bring him over from England than to use a firm from Montreal. My Canadian French was okay for everyday use but I would have struggled with removal jargon.

Phil leaves by train for Halifax the next morning to catch the plane home, and we get ready to leave too. I love the Canadian Pacific locomotives, mighty beasts wreathed in smoke and icicles in Winter, like dragons from the Russian Steppes. We have a wonderful send-off: friends, and a band, hugs, kisses and tears. We had put down roots in a little town on the edge of the sea, amongst miles and miles of spruce trees, now we are pulling them up, and it hurts.

Through the window
I watch leaves make their final landing,
settle on the lawn,
a rust-coloured blanket shaken out by the wind
and flung across the ground.

Behind me is a stripped room,
bare shelves, empty curtain poles,

dust sheets covering the floor.

Exercise book and mouldy paperbacks
lie in untidy heaps
lego men, their faces horribly disfigured by hungry mice,
lie decently buried in plastic bags.

A limp eared one-eyed bear
clings to life,
a rubic cube, a fishing rod, a box marked private,
packed up and ready, labelled "keep"

As the sky darkens,
mirrored in the glass
I meet myself
see a naked light bulb
shine like a moon
in the threadbare trees.

It is time to go.

Jenna Plewes

Stephen and Carol

The rain tumbled down. It didn't merely pelt; it was as though it couldn't wait to get out of the sky, as though it were falling off a shelf. Or off a cliff — Wolf's Crag, maybe. The crematorium was visible in the middle distance, its chimney stilled; but the family had opted for a burial, as befitted a Campbell, albeit an errant one. The family was there, of course, Carol, and Lauren and Greer and Rory. Carol was wearing an astonishing hat over her mass of dyed blond hair; black, naturally, but with feathers and turquoise sequins, which took me back to the time I'd first seen them, her and Stephen, in the village pub.

We'd been there looking for a house; later, it emerged that they had too, but I didn't know that then. I only knew that there was this strange, flamboyant, half-Gothic couple, and I thought maybe village life wouldn't be so bad after all, they had that bohemian manner, that tinge of excess. They were loud, and they treated the place as though it was their own. As English incomers, my wife and I couldn't manage that.

And there were lots of other people there too for the funeral, people I knew, or had known when I still lived there, all subtly transmuted by mourning. Alan, for example, normally the life and soul of the party, but now sombre, tucked away inside himself, uneasy in a shiny suit. The rain came down. The minister intoned. His words were swept away by the wind. The hole gaped; and there were flowers, roses and lilies, for this man who had died in the prime of life — 53, was it? — certainly in the midst of his talent, his paintings becoming better and better known, indeed his vast mural stretching the length of the arrivals lounge at Edinburgh airport.

Not that he was an Edinburgh man; he was a Glasgow man, through and through. An ex-steelworker who had had his real skill discovered under the ever-encouraging auspices of the Glasgow School of Art. And that made me remember another thing: that strange day when he and I and Steve Kempton (I'm going to call Kempton SK from now on) had gone over to the old School. Stephen was to give a guest lecture, but he wasn't quite on message: the lecture, carefully planned — insofar as anything could be carefully planned by Stephen — began and ended with a shot from a starting pistol he'd just bought, astonishingly loud and smokey in the confines of the lecture hall. And afterwards the students crowded around him and complimented him on an amazing lecture; and afterwards we drank vodka; and beforehand we had drunk Special Brew, the three of us, him and me and SK, careening over from the village in Stephen's ancient rattly Land Rover which he should never have driven. Not that it was the driving that killed him.

But on this day, the day of the funeral, we all went back to his house, the little terraced cottage hidden away on the braeside, and there was drinking, but it was decorous and subdued, and I offered my condolences to Carol, as of course I should, because I'd been his best friend in the village (well, me and SK) and that had been for a good twelve years, a long time out of a man's life. And Carol sobbed on my shoulder, and I was pleased to see how well the kids, Lauren and Greer and little Rory, were doing; and then I left the village, for the last time, and flew back down south: feeling melancholy, of course, but it had been a good funeral, a fitting send-off.

The only thing is that of course it didn't happen like that. There's no way it happened like that. I wish it had, but matters are not so simple. I would have loved to go back; I would have loved to 'pay my last respects', as they say. I was genuinely sorry — in fact I was distraught — when I heard that Stephen had died. But I didn't hear that from Carol; I heard it from the village doctor, with whom we'd kept up communication down the years — eight years it was, since we'd left the village.

But much else of what I've said is true. That first scene in the Cross Keys, for example: that was how it was. They were there, and we were there, and let no man tell you otherwise. And also, Stephen was a good artist, you don't need my opinion on that, you can see his work for yourself at any good Scottish gallery — whether he was a great one only time will tell. But there are other parts that need to be filled in, other memories to be arranged, other reasons to be adduced as to why (I think) I wasn't there. Not there at the funeral, I mean; not there amid the tumbling rain.

So. After seeing Stephen and Carol in the pub, we bought our house and moved up, and settled into the life that incomers lead when they settle in a Scottish village. We had a small daughter, and so there was no problem with making school-gate acquaintances, although most of them were younger than we were; and all of them, naturally, were Scottish. There were few other English there, but that didn't prevent us from feeling welcome. Indeed, there were quite a lot of parties, and it was at one of these that I first actually talked to Stephen.

I don't remember the banalities; I remember his quizzical grin, sizing me up, just checking. He smoked cigars; I still had a cigarette habit. He drew me outside; his accent was thick, and it took me a while to understand. That was another thing I never knew: did he put it on for me — not totally, of course, but enough to confound 'Big Dave', as he took to calling me, from down south? There was no telling the limits of his mockery, of his self-irony. He could have been a great man. He was infectious, he was viral, he dominated just by *being*. But.

Out there in the garden at the home of some set of parents of eight-year-olds, I don't recall which, he produced a flask. He offered it to me. Now, I'm not sure what I should say at this stage, because I want you to think of me as a reliable narrator. I don't know why I want that, but I think — I hope — it's not for me, but for Stephen. I want you to know him, but I don't see how I can do that: I don't know whether I knew him myself. I don't know whether his story can ever be told, and, as you will see, I'm certainly not the one to do it.

Anyway, of course he was right, perceptive as always, a man who always went straight to the heart of matters and when there squeezed it brutally. I was drinking heavily in those days — I have what my psychiatrist calls a mild sociophobic disorder — and I accepted the flask with gratitude. And it went on from there. Which of the ensuing events (or habits) shall I describe? Let's start with the old churchyard. The village had a fairly new church; but it had also had an older one, much older, now just a small set of ruins with a large sign tacked to it saying, 'Do not climb', and that was where we so often used to go to set the world to rights; or perhaps just to try to set ourselves to rights; or maybe just to relive our adolescence, I don't know. We used to meet at the Crown (the village had two pubs), late in the evening when the kids, his and mine, had gone to bed; but that was just a prelude really.

He had an old army pack, I remember — he was forever scavenging and scrounging from charity shops — and there would be the cans, and we would down a few and smoke and … well, really, and what? What did we talk about all those nights before we stumbled off back to our long-suffering wives, to Caroline and Carol?

I don't know. It seemed important at the time. But it wasn't only the old churchyard. During the time I was in the village, Stephen and his family moved house several times. For several years they lived in a flat near the village cross, and some high old times we had there, listening to Robert Earl Keen, shouting death to the bourgeoisie, imagining strange deaths and stranger lives. Then came an event which involved villagers with billiard cues — of course — but I don't want to describe that here.

But it does show that there was a dark side. There were phases when he took to phoning me in the middle of the night, leaving huge rambling messages on the answering machine. There were times when there were fresh scars on his already marked face, records of some recent stumble or fall. But beneath all that, that amazing grin — it wasn't a smile, that would be to make it sound too overtly affectionate; it was a grin, worldly-wise and world-weary, but somehow it marked us out as two of a kind, it had that ability, there was something inclusive in it, as though there was a club here, even though it had so desperately few members. All of this was to do with the drink, of course; but I convinced myself it was more than that.

But we weren't actually the only two of a kind: there was SK. He also lived in the village, with his wife Ann. They hated each other. They'd hated each other since — well, you can choose between the two stories. Ann's story was that Steve was permanently drunk, and she'd acted out of desperation; Steve's was that Ann had had an affair and he couldn't get over it. Whatever. Who knows. Steve made an odd living by writing stories for those magazines you always see in the rack in front of you on aeroplanes, but which you only ever pick up in the dead hours of the night on international haul when sleep eludes and death seems very close. I do a lot of that these days.

But Steve was a latecomer, and he was also, sometimes, an early leaver. No stamina, we joked as we collapsed the finished cans, threw them into the undergrowth. No balls — can't even keep his wife. Oh, we were loud jokers then, we were indeed: the world held no terrors for us, staggering round the old graveyard, the crows shouting overhead, the rest of the village cut off in sleep.

I, of course, was relieved by all this: I'd thought that moving to this remote part of the country I'd have to drink on my own. Oh, there was the pub, of course, actually there were, as I've said, two pubs, but that isn't what I mean by drinking: that's just polite consumption, glasses of wine, pints of watered ale. All very nice; but not quite the thing. Not quite the real thing.

Stephen, it seemed to me, was the real thing: a man capable of taking in huge quantities of the strong stuff (though, for some reason I could never quite fathom, he hated whisky) and carrying on. Of course, his mode of carrying on was quite different from my own. I had a job, after all; he had his painting, and in a sense all his time was his own — I envied him this a bit, but I guess I was also aware that it was a danger for him, a terrible danger, all that time, all that waiting for inspiration, all those moments when the vodka bottle might mysteriously appear at your lips.

God, how he would swear at me for a stupid southern wanker if I were to mention that word 'inspiration' — though I often did, mainly to wind him up: in company we fell into role as archetypal Scot and archetypal Anglo as soon as we met. Or maybe after the first couple. He'd have no truck with inspiration: he'd cross his arms — powerful forearms he had, he'd been a steelworker, as I've said: he was short but stocky — and say that painting was *work*, pal, bloody hard work — and it was, I could see that.

Did he have a vision? I don't know. You can go and look, the work is out there. But meanwhile, while you do that, I'm back at the funeral, the funeral that never happened. Oh. You thought I was just saying I hadn't really been there, didn't you? Well, that's true (or as far as you can get in that tricky direction) but as far as I now know there wasn't actually a funeral anyway; just a cremation. Oh, and I don't doubt for a moment that Carol, and the children, were there — of course they were. And I'm sure the people from the village, including Alan and SK, Jane and John Chapman, George and Viv, O'Neill the architect and his mad wife, they were there too. I'm quite sure, yes, I'm quite sure of that. I saw them all. Somehow, I saw them all.

And yet I don't think I was; but let's leave that to one side for a moment, and go back to Stephen and me. He took the piss out of me; mercilessly, for twelve years, he took the piss out of me. But you know, I didn't mind. I was flattered to be in the company of this artist, this maverick, this throwback drinker who could handle as much as I could (well, not quite, but let that be), and whose worldview was coloured by Rimbaud and

Verlaine, by Warhol, even by Blake. What could be better? And besides, I figured his continuing insults were just the outward signs of an affection, a strange affection to be sure, but an affection nonetheless. I don't think I was wrong; but sometimes circumstances are strange.

Oh dear. I hate to say this, but this story is beginning to tire me to tell, and so I'll have to fall back on you, reader. What are you guessing? I can see all kinds of endings to this story. Twelve years drunk in Stephen's company, in the company of the great artist. So: is this a story about repressed homosexuality? Well, since repression is a paradoxical term, there isn't any way of answering that; but I don't think it adds anything to the denouement. Are SK, this mysterious character I've brought on as an also-ran, and the two of us going to get involved in some kind of triangle? Well, we didn't, but there is no doubting that SK was a violent man: there were moments when I felt scared witless of him; God knows about Ann, but he was a different kind of rain, the rain from God. But only occasionally; he could be contained.

Or is this a tedious story about male drinking and the break-up of marriages? Well, unfortunately not, not really: SK's marriage was already broken, Stephen's endured until his death — with, I like to think, a great deal of love on all sides — and mine is intact to this day. So what is it? Don't ask the author (don't *ever* ask the author) but perhaps it's a story about what you don't see: about what's in front of you every day, and you don't see it, you look away, you want to concern yourself with other things.

But to explain that further, I need to turn to Carol. No, this is really important, but please don't jump to conclusions: there was nothing between Carol and me, I was never even sure that she saw me. I mean I'm never sure she saw me, at all. Carol was a Scot of Scots, a Glaswegian among Glaswegians. I don't think she'd ever been down south (though she'd been to the States with Stephen on the occasion of his one and only transatlantic exhibition and its disastrous termination). Her life, her world, was her family: Stephen, of course, and the children, but also a large group of other family members; I don't know who, maybe brothers and sisters, maybe just cousins and aunts. I never knew, but I was aware that Carol *was* her family.

She would go to any lengths to defend them, I remember the night of the first parents' evening at the village school after the arrival of a new headmistress. The school had this thing called the 'Dux Medal' — maybe they were common in Scotland, I had never heard of them down south — which was awarded to the very best-performing pupil in their final year. The new head had tentatively proposed that better educational aims could be achieved by splitting the 'medal' (or rather, the prize) into several parts, so that one child could get a prize for academic attainment, one for good behaviour, one for sport, and so on.

My wife and I arrived in good time for the appointment we had, but we were behind Carol and a friend of hers, so we had to wait outside while we listened to them screaming and shouting at the new head. The gist of their comments was that nobody, especially not an incomer, should tamper with the age-old practices of the school (though they put it more vividly than that). It did occur to me then that Carol had little right to that stance — after all she'd only arrived when we did — although the family of her friend, the wife of a local farmer, had been around for hundreds of years. As had the families of most of the villagers. But I later came to see that Carol had other reasons for clinging to the very particular status of the village.

So. Stephen and I became very close friends; but perhaps that is not the right word, or at least not the best word. Perhaps what we were was accomplices. We liked — this isn't a good admission from someone talking about a time when he was in his forties, is it? — to think of ourselves as outlaws. I remember us doing a strange thing in the village. Through Stephen's connections on the art scene, we managed to get a grant, quite a decent grant, to provide village youth — not only from our village, but from others around — with opportunities to paint; to watch film; to sculpt; generally hang out with other kinds who were interested in art but didn't often have the opportunity to travel into the nearby towns.

I won't say it was a raging success; but it certainly challenged the village, not least because of Stephen's insistence that for the kids to really learn there had to be life drawing. Since we couldn't afford professional models, this involved Stephen finding some girl who would take her clothes off and lie on the floor of the village hall (not a nice prospect) while a group of inexperienced youths clustered around her and made amateurish daubs on their cheap canvases. Strange rumours spread, of course, but I can assure you it was all perfectly above board. I expect you believe me. And I still like to think that the village youth benefited from seeing the early films of Kenneth Anger; certainly it was difficult enough to get hold of copies of them — that was my role.

But when I say 'challenged', of course the village manifested a contradictory attitude to Stephen. You'd expect it, wouldn't you? Here's this eminent artist, come to settle among us —

and although he's an incomer, he's a Glasgow incomer, so we can live with that. And he's got three children, and we can live with those. And — well — he's got a drink problem, but we can live with that too. In fact, Forrester at the Crown and Angus up at the Cross Keys would have a hard old time of it overall if there wasn't one or two … Far more there were than one or two, including the farmer's wife who drowned herself in Loch Laggan, but we needn't go into that now. Though what did she remember, I wonder, those last minutes amid the pines that ran down to the water — there were no alders there, although I remember the Scottish alders, they only really thrive in fast-flowing water, and the water in Loch Laggan was still, perfectly still; except for that splash, which the deer barely noticed. A perfect death, a terrible death: nobody understood, her husband never understood, why. No obvious history of depression, no outward sign: a sudden commitment one night, out of the blue, death by water.

Which brings me by a strange route back to the funeral. That funeral. Stephen's funeral. And whether I was there. I've already said that I heard about it — about Stephen's death, I mean, as well as the funeral — at second hand, and here is where the memory grows difficult. There were three days to go: I could go, I should go, it wouldn't be difficult to go, there are planes from where I live now to Edinburgh, only takes an hour, and then another hour by train and then a bus-ride — or a taxi, I can afford it.

What do I do? What did I do? It had been eight years since I'd seen Stephen. I'd half-thought, when I left Scotland, that our friendship — if that was what it was — might continue, but really I'd recognised that it was … what's the right word? Circumstantial? There we'd been together, but what would be the value of such a friendship, the content of it, if we were separated by five hundred miles, if we could no longer spend nights under the shadow of the ruins of the old church, if we could no longer see ourselves as somehow separate and yet belonging? How would it work?

It hadn't. He'd never contacted me again, and I formed a view on that. Looking back now, I'm no longer sure it was the right view; certainly it wasn't the most relevant one. The view was that these things didn't travel: it was an episode, perhaps even a strange kind of dream, from which I'd woken up. And I had woken up from it: I've never since sought out drinking partners — sentimentally, I thought, nobody could replace Stephen; realistically, a deeper part of my brain, or more probably my body, supplied the missing link by reminding me that if ever I did again, I would probably die an untimely death. Which I haven't; but Stephen did. I remember a time he was hospitalised (not the only one) and Carol (so he said afterwards) used to bring him in supplies of vodka disguised in his favourite hot water bottle. I'd prefer not to go that way.

Anyway. It would be nice to conclude this story with a conversation, and I'm going to, it seems necessary. The pity of it is that I would have liked it to be face-to-face, person-to-person, but it wasn't. At least, I'm pretty sure it wasn't. Let's accept for now that I didn't go the funeral, and that this alternative version of things took place; though I'm not sure. I heard about Stephen's death on a Friday; the cremation was to be on the Tuesday. Over the weekend, I dithered. I didn't know what I wanted: I was in a busy period of writing, my older daughter was visiting, I hadn't, for God's sake, seen Stephen for years. What should I do?

On the Sunday evening, I decided I would have to phone. Obviously I'd have to, because I didn't know exactly where the ceremony was going to take place. So I phoned Carol. I was primed to offer my condolences; I just wanted to ask about the details, establish the time and place, and then, I thought, I'd book a flight and wing my way up on the Tuesday morning, or Monday night if need be.

I didn't get Carol. I got a female voice alright, but it wasn't Carol, and I didn't recognise it. I said who I was, and I asked who she was, and there was a moment of silence. 'Lauren', she said — Stephen's eldest. I tried madly to calculate how old she would be now — in her early twenties, I supposed. Her voice was frosty.

I said, "I was wanting to come up for the funeral, and wondering what time it is ..." — my voice faltered, it was as though I could hear the silence at the other end of the line.

"He'd not have been dead", she said; for a moment I misheard her, and thought she was saying that he wasn't dead, my mind did a somersault, and I made no reply, and she went on.

"You'll not be welcome", she said, "because it if wasn't for you he'd not have been dead".

I found it hard to believe what I was hearing. "I'm taking the phone in the other room", said Lauren. I tried to picture her, but it had been eight years. Red hair, for sure, and thin; but beyond that ...

"Mum was expecting you to phone", said Lauren, "and I'm to tell you this. Some of it's before my time, but she wants you to know. OK?"

She sounded determined, although I had no idea what was going on. "OK", I said.

"Mum says to tell you that we all moved out of Glasgow twenty years ago, and that she wants you to tell me why that was".

I racked my brains. "How can I know", I asked, "I didn't know any of you until you moved to the village".

"Guess", said Lauren, and I knew then that she'd moved away from her mum's script to her own, to the script of a bereaved daughter. I swallowed. I hadn't really thought of it before.

"Well", I said, "your father was not a cautious man. I imagine it might have been felt that in a small village ..."

"With less temptations", Lauren supplied.

"Yes, I suppose so", I said, and all at once I saw where this conversation was going, but I had no chance to say so.

"But then", Lauren said, "he met you. Within a few weeks, wasn't it? So I'm told. And there he is, back on the bottle, and with a lovely friend to drink with. Except that when he comes home, he's not so lovely. He's not lovely at all. It's not that my dad was a brute; he was a wonderful man. But when he was drunk, he was a brute. He was a brute to me, and to Greer and to Rory, and to my mum. He would stagger in through the door — and I remember this myself — often having pissed against it — and he'd stumble over the kitchen table, and often as not he'd shout and rave, and ..."

I'd had enough of this, and shouted in my turn. "And this is my fault? Your father was an alcoholic, and he died of it, didn't he?" I had no idea whether this was medically true, but the general conclusion seemed inescapable.

"Oh yes", said Lauren quietly, "that's all true. But my mum brought him out of Glasgow to this quiet place so that he could recover, so that he could be away from his drinking companions, and look at what we got. What we got was you".

I don't remember what she said after that. I was upset. I don't know what I did either.

Anyway, what I have to comfort me is the memory of the funeral, of the coffin being gently lowered. I remember those six stout men — SK among them, of course, and Alan, and the tremulous slide of the ropes as the coffin begins its descent. I remember being there, silently paying homage to Stephen. I don't think I caused it, did I? After all, he was always on skid row. And I am not, so there's a blessing, if of an infamous kind. I think I'm being blamed for something I never caused. I can feel the rain; I can hear the wind blowing off Wolf's Craig. I can hear Stephen's voice, saying, "Big Dave, big Dave". I can hear his mockery, so violent, so tender. I was his best friend during those years, and so it's fitting that I'm here, at his funeral, even many days, many years after the event. I need, after all, to pay my respects. I shall, I think, always be here.

David Punter

The Seventh Magpie

Folk superstition says seeing a lone magpie brings bad luck. To fend off misfortune, in Britain people used to doff their hat to a lone magpie, greet it politely, or wave their arms to imitate a second magpie as two magpies meant joy or good luck. A popular rhyme (with many regional variations) tells that seeing a certain number of magpies can predict or influence the future:

> *One for sorrow, two for mirth,*
> *Three for a wedding, four for a birth,*
> *Five for silver, six for gold,*
> *Seven for a secret not to be told,*

One for sorrow, two for mirth

On the day of Martha's burial, as the coffin was being lowered, her husband Harry stamped the ground and was heard to emit strange cries, taken by mourners to be sounds of grief struggling from his throat. Afterwards, at the wake in the pub, Martha's brother Pete pronounced the cries were not Harry's but came from the black and white bird landing on the coffin before flapping into the trees.

"I saw Harry shoo the bird off, arms like propellers," Pete waved his arms to demonstrate, and tottered, his beer splashing on the counter.

The others in the pub laughed, "Is that right, Harry? We saw no bird. Too busy gabbing we were." The pub landlord leaned across to Harry, "Pete here says you chased it off. Not doing harm was it? Just the one bird, eh?"

Harry picked up another sandwich, tore off the crust and looked at the ceiling. "Saw one, saw more. There were others."

"You did not so," Harry's mother, Joan, broke in, "with your face buried in my hankie! You were blubbing away summat fierce, wouldn't have seen anything. Birds!"

Pete held up his beer and whooped, "Wahey, matey, not one but lots! Whaddasay? What a racket up in the trees, eh Harry, caw caw?"

The small crowd all turned to Harry who was chewing very slowly, not looking at anyone. At this moment he hated them all, particularly Pete. "The funeral was bad enough," he muttered to himself, "now got to listen to this crowd of wankers."

"Cackling," he said at last, "yeah, that's what they were doing, cackling away."

Joan burped and giggled. "Funny business, all said and done," she ventured, wafting away a fly, "birds cackling at a funeral. Like they was having a laugh."

Three for a wedding, four for a birth

On Martha's big day it had rained all morning. She sighed and wondered if galoshes or boots would be too out of place with her wedding gown, or should she just accept the disaster-in-waiting and wear the satin stilettos. She pictured them rain-soaked and ruined. "Hell, no one's gonna look under the gown at my feet, are they?" She stared at herself in the mirror, "I could change boots real quick, at the door before the march down the aisle. While folk are shaking umbrellas. Mmmm, that's it." Martha turned sideways to check if her bulge showed too much. "Four more hours, then I will be a proper missus, Mrs Henry Ostwhittle. Tongue-twister, that; takes a bit getting used to. Mr and Mrs Ostwhittle, husband and wife." She stroked her abdomen. "And baby makes three."

It had been natural to get together, Harry had reasoned. Though they'd never been school sweethearts, they had known each other from primary school. Two misfit kids, mates through mutual shyness he admitted to himself as he selected a tie and checked his posture in the mirror. The wedding cars were booked and Joan was scurrying about annoyingly with his ironed shirt and new trousers. "Got to look your best before the bride," she smiled. Harry sighed. He was pleased now about the baby despite the shock. Everything was so unexpected. Martha had egged him on that summer in the house alone, and he'd been too scared to let on he was still a virgin, but somehow they found how things worked and the deed was done. And now Martha being pregnant was blamed on him for being careless, or as Martha's brother put it, 'bloody stupid'. After the shouting had died down, Pete had a man-to-man with Harry, and Harry did the decent thing. The day he proposed, Harry told Martha he had come across a huge nest in the overgrown hawthorn tree he was planning to chop down. "Guess what, that nest's got a baby chick hatched, all fluffy, and there's another egg waiting," he had said, "and the parents diving and chittering to scare me off. Guess I'll leave the tree alone for a while." After they settled in his mother's house Harry knew Joan would help out with babysitting, and he would be free to make better use of the garden, grow tomatoes or whatever.

Martha checked herself in the mirror again. "Big magpies he said they were. Magpies. Wonder if that other egg hatched." She wrapped her wedding shoes in a plastic bag and rummaged in the wardrobe for decent boots. "Birds were chattering in that tree again this morning. Harry says it's the same ones, two chicks and the pair. Don't know how long they live. I think Harry said years." Martha straightened up and felt the baby kick. "Don't care if it shows," she smiled, "just three months to go, that's all, then a chick of our own."

Five for silver, six for gold

Joan turned to her son, with a sly smile on her face. "She's up to something," Harry thought, heaving himself out of the armchair. He was feeling tired, having been up most of the night with the baby, his turn while Martha slept. For a premmie the kid was doing OK he reckoned, just not sleeping well. Who does these days? He grimaced and yawned.

"Brought you a little prezzie Martha might like," Joan said, holding out a small pink box. "It's what my mother gave me when I got married." She took out a small object wrapped in tissue, "it's a brooch, see!" Harry looked and made out he was thrilled. Joan held it to the light, "all real silver. See the cute design in the middle? Five lovebirds on a tiny branch. Can't tell if they're doves or not. Just needs a bit of a polish." She put the brooch back in the box. "Silver's gone a bit tarnished, makes the birds look dark, not like lovebirds at all, more like those effing magpies in your garden!" Harry watched as his mother twirled and skipped around the room with the box. She sure knows how to irritate me, he thought. She could've waited and given Martha the brooch after the wedding. Now, a year later, it'll seem like a poor afterthought.

He sighed, "yeah, Mum, I guess it'll be right up Martha's street, she'll love it." Joan gave a chirp of delight, "I knew it, she's got my style." He and Martha had only been married twelve months, but what with the baby not sleeping, and his mother always messing about, he felt grumpy and depressed. He reckoned he and Martha were going through what people call 'a bad patch'. Martha had gone off sex, always too tired or not feeling well. Harry wondered if she still loved him, or were they just bored with each other. He must have said something to Martha's brother, for Pete had declared all new marriages go through a bad patch. He said he'd been through the same with his missus, and clapped him on the shoulder, "chin up, matey!"

Harry sat back down in the chair and almost nodded off when Joan trotted in with the silver polish and a rag he recognised as a remnant of one of his old shirts. "Now let's see it in all its glory," she said as she got to work. Harry yawned again. The smell of the silver polish was making him feel sick, and he got up.

"Hang on," Joan held the brooch out. "Look at what's come up, the branch's shaped like a small bird, and the branch isn't silver, it's gold! That counts as six lovebirds, I remember now. Mum always said birds had to be in pairs. Clear slipped my mind."

Harry took the brooch and rocked it in the palm of his hand. "Might be worth a few bob," he thought.

In the year before Martha got the cancer that killed her, Harry found love. She was the cleaner Joan had hired for them when Martha got too poorly to do the heavy housework. Harry smiled. Twyla her name was. He remembered thinking the name was really pretty. She was pretty too. Twyla had a twinkly smile Harry found irresistible. She would be bending down to dust or polish something and then peek round her shoulder at him watching her and give a big smile. Martha like her too, Harry thought, she was a good worker. Sometimes Twyla teased him, pretending to chase him with the vacuum cleaner. Harry shut his eyes against the memory. "Too bad. Everything at the wrong time. Story of my life." He blew his nose and looked round at the assembled mourners by the grave. "But I reckon Martha knew, but never said. The way Martha looked at me when Twyla was around. No, I never told. Not that we did any wrong."

Harry walked a few feet away from the rest, and watched the preparations for the lowering of the coffin. "Cuddles was all ever happened. Just kissing."

He looked up again at the trees at the edge of the cemetery and remembered Twyla going into the garden to throw stale bread to the birds and the funny little dances she did under the hawthorn tree. It was when Twyla told him she wasn't dancing but had to flap her arms whenever she saw a lone magpie and call out 'hello Mr Magpie, how is your family today?' that he fell in love. At that moment he felt himself the lone magpie and wished he could take Twyla in his arms and hold her tight. "You see, one magpie shouldn't be alone, so I show him I'm Mrs Magpie," Twyla had earnestly explained, "so he thinks here is another magpie, and then he isn't lonely and he brings me luck."

Harry shook his head. Not that he stopped loving Martha, but this had been so different, this sudden madness he couldn't control. He lived for the secret embraces and hugs, his breath trembling afterwards. He knew Twyla didn't feel the same way but she had let him kiss her. For that he was grateful.

Then Martha died and Twyla went. Joan had said Twyla had given in her notice saying there was no longer any need for her to come to the house. Her goodbye to Harry had been brief and business-like. He had felt devastated. Harry gazed at the last of the people slowly ambling out of the church. Did Twyla come to the funeral? Harry thought he'd caught sight of her earlier in the church, but maybe imagined that. He discovered he was crying and choked back a loud sob. His mother pushed a hankie into his hand. Harry lurched, startled. "Leave off, will you!" He stamped on a small pile of loose soil by the grave and kicked a stone. "Still love her," he muttered to himself, "told her as much the day she left."

A small group of mourners were chatting among themselves, and Pete signalled to him to come over. Harry pretended he did not see and wiped his face, but Pete still persisted, waving both arms. Harry walked over, feeling defeated as Pete patted his back. "Hey, matey, it'll be all right, you've got family. Won't let you down."

A clutch of birds took off from the trees, screeching as Martha's coffin was lowered. "Damn magpies," Harry blurted out, "keep following me around. Look at them. Seven of the buggers now squawking away. Same three pairs as what's in our garden I bet, and that little one on his own." He suddenly felt faint, swayed and buried his face into the handkerchief. Joan tiptoed up. "You all right, love?"

Harry turned, pointing to the small magpie just landing on the coffin. "That's the one alone," he cried, "the one on his own", and raising his arms like giant wings, flapped and flapped and flapped.

Greta Ross

Survival

As the black water swept up and around Sam's knees he knew the trawler was going down. The next gust slammed the boat against a mountain of solid sea.

A flash of lightning. His father at the radio, shouting — the mayday, the coordinates, the panic, were buried in the deafening roar of the wind, a furious train passing in the sky above. And then the shriek of splitting wood. The boat leaned further.

Where's Jimmy?

Lights were still working down below, an otherworldly glow from the water that was quickly rising, Jimmy wading in it almost to his chest, trying to drag out the survival suits. No time for that now. They'd made mistakes. Sam stepped down and pulled his brother away, pushed him up the companionway. The old man was struggling to hold on. He pushed Jimmy toward their father and pointed.

Help him.

Another mistake. Stubborn old man always insisted on coming out every time, like he didn't trust them even after all these years. Sam hoped there would be a chance to argue with him about it again.

The life-raft canister, bolted to the deck, was open and Sam felt a fleeting moment of relief just seeing it. He reached in to pull out the raft. Another wave hit, another monster, and he choked on water — had the boat gone under? — felt himself lifted, swept off his feet, scrambling, then found his feet again. Still on deck.

But something was wrong. One of the outriggers had collapsed and smashed the canister lid down onto his hand. He couldn't lift it. He was stuck. Water surged to his waist.

Jimmy held onto the old man and together the three of them shifted the boom and managed to lift the lid. Sam was free. As they hauled out the life-raft, the boat fell away. The old man was thrown and Jimmy leapt to grab him. Sam saw the life-raft fly overboard.

There was no thinking. He threw himself after it.

There was a long, terrible moment of deathlike black and cold and searing pain in his chest. He couldn't tell which way was up, then found the surface and air — and vomited water. Just ahead of him the life-raft inflated.

He didn't remember climbing in but he was there; he could breathe and he held on as the sea tried to toss him out, again and again. In a moment the others would come. He searched the water. The running lights were submerged and the night was black, but in the flashes of lightning he could see — nothing. Nothing but treacherous sea. In the final rending, the ripping and the screaming wind, he heard their voices. And there! His father and Jimmy, clinging to the wreckage as it went down, calling to him. He reached for an oar but his hand, his fingers weren't working. He tried, but the oar chopped uselessly then was ripped from his hand, and the waves and the wind dragged him further away.

Paralyzed, possessed by terror, he watched the ending as it all went under and was gone. And still he could hear them calling his name, begging him to come back. He could do nothing. The raft swept him away and the voices faded into the clamor of the storm.

✵

Sam wondered if this was death. Maybe hell. The sea was a demon and laid siege through the night and all through the next day, trying to finish the job it had started. The forces clawed at him with purpose, tipping the raft on edge. He gagged and vomited endlessly. He tried to erect the canopy, impossible in the storm with one hand useless. He used his good hand to bail and had time for nothing else. Everything was cold and fear and pain; if he didn't struggle, if he didn't continue to bail, it would all stop. It would be over. But he bailed. And still he heard their voices. The long black day turned into black night and the storm continued.

Exhaustion won. He somehow fell asleep and when he woke up on the second day it was over and he wasn't dead.

The sun had been up long enough that his life vest and shirt were almost dry, though his pants, sitting in seawater in the bottom of the raft, were soaked. When he tried to sit up he realized he was tied to the grab lines with a rope. He didn't remember doing that. The same rope was also tied around his wrist and around his right hand, around and around, so tight that his hand was numb. He didn't remember doing that either. The hand was sticky and oozed blood. He looked at it with indifference. He needed water.

Every move hurt, every muscle. His lips and tongue cracked with dried salt. There were four small bottles of water in the storage well and he drank two of them down without pause, without thinking, and felt no relief so he drank a third. A nugget of common sense stopped him before he opened the fourth.

The sea, angry dark, rolled in large swells. The horizon was clear and empty in all directions. Fear welled in him like a choke-hold and he had to gasp to get air.

The lid of the raft canister had slammed down on his hand — that he remembered — but he didn't remember feeling pain. He didn't expect to see his fingers fall away as he unwrapped the rope tourniquet. A torrent of fresh blood pumped into his lap.

Stunned, he pulled the rope tight again. The three middle fingers weren't completely severed, but hung on unconvincingly with tendons and shreds of muscle. New pain slammed him as the blood seeped back into his hand, into the stumps where splintered, flesh-specked bone protruded like a nightmare.

There was a horrible sound, a bellow that he knew must be his own but sounded inhuman. If he could have run like a panicked wildebeest he would have. But he remained trapped in the small rubber boat, surrounded by the hateful sea. It had taken people he loved, drowned them before his eyes as they pleaded for him to come back. He was lost. He was alone. His hand was mangled. And he was desperately thirsty.

He wept for a long time and felt the tears drain his body.

Did he want to live? He thought of his mother. Her husband and youngest son were dead — would it matter to her that she had one son left? He dreaded the idea of having to face her.

Did he care about seeing his friends again? Did he care about seeing his indifferent girlfriend? Not really. It would be easy to just lie there and be thirsty, let his wound fester. To go to sleep forever.

The hard thing to do, the most frightening thing, would be to fight. To live.

*

A scream woke him — a seagull dipping close to check him out. His thirst was now unbearable. He opened the last bottle and took just one mouthful. It was worse than none at all. It was torture. He had to urinate badly, but had no energy, no will, to kneel and go over the side. Or maybe to pee into a bottle. He didn't care and just let it go, sitting where he was, and it warmed him and even amused him to think that he was literally pissing away his life.

At the end of his right arm was a throbbing lump of flesh still wrapped in filthy rope, still seeping blood. Rummaging through the storage pockets, he found a first aid kit with gauze and ointment. And a packet of blades. He pulled the rope tighter around his wrist and picked at the gummy mess to untangled the fingers. They were swollen and ghastly white, like dead fish belly.

Impossible to muster enough strength to lift his arm, to dip his hand into the sea. But it had to be done. The fingers wobbled in the water like squid bait and he wondered if he could catch something to eat. That made him laugh.

Awkwardly one-handed, with help from his teeth, he ripped strips of gauze and tied tourniquets around the stump of each dead finger. When he released the rope around his wrist his hand stung painfully as it came back to life. He tried to push the fingers back on with some desperate hope they could be saved. Maybe if he wrapped them up. Maybe if he got rescued soon — that other pressing problem. But the fingers were lifeless, clearly no longer part of him.

He picked up a blade. It didn't hurt. It didn't even take courage. He did it and threw them into the sea.

Dribbling precious drops of water from the last bottle, he carefully cleaned the wounds and smeared them with ointment. Then he slowly and deliberately drank the rest of the water.

So many mistakes. Goddamn his father for not listening to their ideas to improve the boat, to modernize. He was too goddamn old.

Sam sobbed once and shivered. The sun was behind clouds and he was chilled, so he pulled a tarp around himself to get warm.

＊

Another scream woke him. This time not a gull.

He'd slumped into the bottom of the raft, and when he sat up he couldn't remember where he was. The sound had been real and very loud, a shriek, but there was nothing there. He couldn't remember why he was in a life-raft. Dreaming, he imagined. His head throbbed. He was hot and very thirsty.

There is no water.

Why was there no water? He needed a drink. He couldn't understand why he was here. He was *too hot*. When he pushed away the tarp he saw his bandaged hand and remembered.

Delirium had been so much better.

Then it came again, behind him. A blast. He turned and saw a tanker, huge and not far off, coming toward him. It was a few long moments before he could place himself, before he could remember why this was important.

There were flares in the storage. He pulled them out and struggled to open the case. His hand was shaking badly. He could barely breathe, thought he might pass out. He got out the gun — orange plastic — and fumbled it, dropped it.

Hurry.

The ship was already passing before him. Close enough to smell diesel. Close enough to hear the engines. And then he saw a man on deck, looking right at him

Hurry!

He reached for the gun but couldn't break it open. Got it open, reached for the cartridge. Only one shaking hand — how could he load the cartridge? He struggled, looked up; the man was still looking right at him. With binoculars.

The cartridge fell. The gun fell. Sam looked at the man and held his arms wide open.

Help.

The man walked away.

Sam waited. The tanker passed. He waited for it to slow, to stop, to turn back. The tanker disappeared.

*

It had never been there. He realized he was suffering from severe dehydration. The confusion. The shakes. The pounding head. While he'd slept, wrapped in the tarp, the sun had come out and he'd sweated out the final drops of moisture he could spare. He expected death would come soon. He felt hot. He felt chilled, feverish. His hand must be festering, infection racing through to his heart. He closed his eyes and let himself go.

Very clearly, as if they were sitting just out there riding the waves, he could hear his father, he could hear Jimmy, calling his name. But this time they didn't sound scared. They were cheerful. It sounded like a party and they were calling Sam to come along. The music was loud.

A blast. Very loud drumming. And shouting. And the smell of diesel.

He opened his eyes.

The tanker was back. It filled the sky. There were men on deck, running and yelling and waving to him.

Is this real?

He couldn't move. A boat was lowered over the side of the ship; it hit the water and in moments they were there, arms around him, pulling him up. Wrapping him. Lifting him.

He couldn't understand what they were saying. He couldn't speak. All he could do was cry, but he had no tears.

Debra Tillar

Applause

"Ladies and Gentlemen . . . Billy Manners!"

He struts onto the stage, the clapping and shouting of a thousand fans roll over him like a warm wave. In the wings, he performed his usual routine — counting to ten and taking a deep breath, then slapping on a smile before stepping out. There is no turning back, no way to slip into the quiet of his dressing room and slug the vodka he keeps in his bag. As usual, the faces are indiscernible in the lowered houselights — silhouettes, ghosts — and he sometimes wishes he could see who they are, know something about them and their lives. But that's not what he is paid to do, not the path he has taken. For several decades, he's performed in front of nameless crowds who laugh and applaud, not a single audience member ever really knowing who he is, even though they read about him in magazines or see him in interviews. This is the life he chose. The only life he could have chosen.

He steps into the spotlight and grabs the mic.

"Hello, San Jose!"

The crowd cheers.

"So nice to be back here in the Silicon Valley, which I think was named because of all the tech giants and not the giant tits scattered throughout the audience."

The first break of laughter.

"I'm not a tit man."

Scattered chuckles.

"I see some of you read."

More chuckles.

"The last time I saw a boob I was six months old, and my mother was complaining, 'How much longer do I have to do this?'"

Laughter from the audience. He lowers his voice for effect.

"I held on for another year."

More laughter and some applause.

"Hey! It was like half-and-half!"

He waits as the laughter dies down.

"You straight guys out there who have a breast fixation — you know what that means? You might have an undetected Vitamin D deficiency."

More laughter. Inside, he wrestles with phantom images, trying to stay on track, keep the bits going in his head. He clamps down, pushes on.

❁

Comics aren't born, they are made — forged by forces beyond their control. Laughter is a survivor's tool, his comedy coach once said, the hammer that lets you pound your way through life's obstacles. And Billy learned how to wield it, make money with it.

As a child, he'd hid in his room, avoiding the war zone that was his parents' marriage — his dad an alcoholic with a gambling problem and perennial five o'clock shadow who only sometimes made it home on Fridays; his mother a philandering waitress who tended toward plunging necklines and swing shifts so that she could be late coming home. From the confines of his ten-by-ten bedroom, he covered his ears with his hands — shut out the rest of his house as best he could, sometimes burying his face in his pillow.

"Out whoring around?" his dad's voice slurred.

"Oh, stick your whiskey bottle up your ass!"

He imagined his mother's face twisted into a mocking expression, lip curled up on one side — his dad's eyes red-rimmed, his mouth drawn in a constant state of depression mixed with anger. Then the slapping started, the thuds of fists, the throwing of objects, and he knew that the next day someone would be bruised, maybe bandaged. He wondered if the cops would come again.

He ran away once — and not successfully. How far could a five-year-old get? He had no money and in a paper sack he carried nothing but two pairs of underwear, a pair of socks, and a peanut butter sandwich he'd made. He made it down the street and past the school where he attended kindergarten. He hid in the large juniper bushes that hugged the front and side of the school, their branches scraping at his face and arms as he crawled through the tangle of gin-berry smelling boughs. He would have spent the night there and planned his move for the next day, but the school's janitor, Charlie, saw him disappear into the greenery.

"Billy? Billy Manners, is that you in those bushes?"

He stayed quiet, but a sudden sneeze gave him away.

"What are you doing in there?" Pause. "Do I need to call your parents?"

"No!" he shouted. "I don't want to go home!"

"Why the heck not?"

"Because."

"Because why?"

"It's scary there."

Charlie eventually managed to coax him out, brushed off dirt and dried juniper needles from his clothes, and then walked him to the teacher's lounge where he took his coffee and dinner breaks. He offered Billy a Coke and helped him into a chair.

"Now, you tell me," he said, "what's so scary about home?"

Billy sat there, staring at the floor. After a minute, he said, "My parents fight all the time."

"Fight how?"

He looked up at the janitor, eyes glistening. He wiped at the tears with the back of his hand. "They yell and scream. Sometimes they hit each other."

Charlie's eyes widened. "They do?"

"Yeah. Not like on TV."

It was 1965 and Billy's only references for families were the Cleavers and Andy Griffith's household. The janitor scooted his chair closer and placed both hands on Billy's shoulders. Being a five-year-old, Billy had no idea how tall or how old the man was. His hair was thin and mostly gray, and he spoke with an accent, like someone from another country.

"Those TV families are made up. In real life, we don't always get the families we want." Charlie spoke in low tones, like he didn't want anyone else to hear, even though only he and Billy were there. "And sometimes we have to deal with what we have. It makes us stronger." He paused. "Are there ever any good times in your home?"

"Sometimes."

"Tell me."

Billy told him about the time they went on a car trip to the coast. Monterey. He got to see seals and otters, and then they went to the Aquarium.

"Well, that sounds like a great trip," Charlie said.

Billy nodded again, his eyes now dry.

"Know what you need to do?"

Billy shook his head.

"When it gets bad in your house, you think of that time in Monterey. Think about the seals, the otters, and all the great animals you saw at the Aquarium. Think of other times when you had fun." He pointed several times at Billy's face. "You close your eyes, and you remember all that good stuff."

Billy just looked at him.

"Believe me, it helps." The janitor pulled back. "And, well, you can always come and visit me here at school. I could always use someone to help me clean erasers."

Billy beamed. "Really?"

"Sure." He stood. "Now, let's get you home."

"There's no one there," Billy said.

Charlie scrunched his face. "But it's five o'clock!"

"My mom works at night and my dad doesn't come home sometimes."

"And they leave you there alone?"

Billy nodded again. "It's not so bad. It's quiet. I just watch TV or read."

The janitor rubbed his chin. "Well, let's call your home and see."

Billy knew his phone number by heart and waited while the janitor dialed. After a minute or so, he hung up.

"Yep. Nobody answers." He put his hands on his hips and looked down at Billy. "Well, looks like you're going to have to hang out with me for a while."

Billy stayed with him until the janitor located his father several hours later. Every school day after that, Billy delayed going home and kept Charlie company until his friend said it was time for him to skedaddle, and then he would trudge down the street with his head down. He cried in the fourth grade when his teacher told him the janitor had died from a heart attack the night before. The last thing he remembered Charlie saying to him was, "You're a smart kid. The teachers say you are. I know you'll be something someday. Probably famous." He tousled Billy's hair and then whistled as he pushed his dust-mop around and Billy cleaned erasers and whistled too.

❖

"You may have heard I turned fifty recently."

The crowd erupts into applause.

"Thank you, thank you. It didn't bother me. I mean, isn't fifty the new forty?"

A few cheers and shouts from the audience.

"I did go over the edge one morning, though. It happened on the toilet."

Members of the audience chuckle as he drops to a semi squat, as though sitting down on the john.

"I know some of you men out there have had this terrifying experience."

Some anticipatory laughs. He hums and then casually looks down between his legs. He jerks his head up, eyes wide. Then his expression melts into fake distress as he cries out, "I have a white ball hair!"

The crowd breaks into a wave of laughter.

"Yeah. You older guys know what I'm talking about. That day you discover that your balls need Just for Men."

Scattered laughter.

"So I did what any red-blooded gay American male would do." Pause. "I shaved the boys."

More chuckles.

"Now, if you have not yet taken the step toward manscaping, let me give you these words of advice. First, make sure your razor is clean and fresh."

People listen intently. Someone coughs.

"Second, do the shave in the shower with warm water and plenty of soap." Another pause. "And third, make sure you've taken your allergy medicine. Because the last thing you want to do is sneeze in the middle of the process."

He acts out a sneeze while his hand gestures the slicing of the razor near his genitals and cries out in pain as he limps around the stage. The audience breaks into a combination of laughter and applause.

"I had a friend who went into a sneezing fit and now serves as a backup voice for Dora the Explorer."

Some people laugh so hard he hears chortling.

"The problem with shaving is how quickly it grows back. And the white hairs seem to multiply. Pretty soon your balls look like two raspberries left in the fridge too long."

He waits for the laughter to subside.

"So a good friend recommended I try something else." Pause. He holds up his finger like he's announcing something. "Ball waxing!"

Some men in the audience groan. Other audience members laugh. For a moment he thinks. He knows where this bit is going, how he will make fun of the physical pain and induce guffaws from the assemblage. And for a split second, he wishes that all pain could be so funny.

❧

The first time Billy was beaten up for being gay was in middle school. By that time his parents had split up. His dad moved to his home state of Ohio and died in a car accident late one night. He'd been driving drunk, lost control, and the car plunged into a small lake. The vehicle glug-glugged its way to the bottom and his father wasn't found for three days. Billy didn't cry. His mom took up with a man who had frequented the restaurant where she worked. His name was Joe, and he was a transplant from England with no formal education who painted houses for a living. He teased Billy for being a bookworm, for reading European folk tales and stories of Greek myths.

"Get outside and get your hands dirty," he sometimes said. "Learn to be a man, not a pansy."

Billy winced at the word. He was slight of build, destined not to be much taller than five-feet-six, short genes running on both sides of the family. He didn't walk or talk like a girl, at least he didn't think so. But he didn't play sports of any kind, didn't much care to watch them on TV, and was prone to spending time alone — a habit he carried over from his earlier childhood. Yet something gnawed at him on the inside. Somehow, he was different.

In the eighth grade, Billy developed a crush on David Allman, a blond baseball-playing classmate with eyes that radiated hues from the bluest parts of the Pacific. He lost concentration in class at times as his gaze wandered from the teacher to linger on David — wondering what his life was like, wondering what his favorite food was, wondering what he looked like naked. Billy had always noticed other boys since the first grade, watched them play or joke at recess or lunchtime. But he was thirteen now — and with David, his heart quickened as he eyed the other boy walk down the hallway. His groin stirred as he sat on the bleachers, pretending to read while secretly watching David stand at the plate, bat in hand, crouched with legs slightly spread. And at night, his dreams went to places he never conjured during the day.

Billy's locker was only five down from David's. One day, after the last class bell had rung, he asked him if he wanted to work on their social studies project together.

"Sure," David said. "You're the smartest kid here. I could use the help."

He smiled as he said this, and Billy felt the stirring, the desire to reach out and touch the other boy's face, trace his lips with his fingertips.

After two sessions of working together, Billy mustered up his courage. David had been looking over his shoulder, his breath warm on Billy's neck. He rubbed Billy on the head and said, "I'm glad I'm working with you." Then he sauntered over to the bed and sat, leaving Billy at his desk. He put his pen down and looked over at David, who sat there, book open, taking notes.

"I was wondering," Billy said, "is there anyone at school you like?"

"What do you mean?"

Billy felt heat in his cheeks. "I mean, anyone you're interested in?"

David shook his head. "Not really. Why?" He looked up.

"Because — because —" Billy cleared his throat. "I have a crush on someone."

"Who?"

Billy took in a deep breath and exhaled. He looked directly at the other boy. "You," he said softly.

Something flashed in those sapphire eyes of his study companion. They opened wide for just a moment and then narrowed, lasering their focus as an emotion deep from David's gut pushed to get out. Billy realized it wasn't joy or even surprise.

"I'm not a homo!" David jumped up and hurriedly stuffed things into his backpack. "You stay away from me!"

And before Billy thought about what to say, what he should do, David stormed out of the room, the front door slamming as he left. Billy sat at his desk, gaze lowered, his eyes glistening. What had he done? Why hadn't he kept his feelings to himself? He stood and traipsed to the bed and plopped down. He placed his hand where David had sat, the bed still warm. He brushed the cover lightly with his fingers, then brought the hand to his mouth in a gentle caress. He stared at nothing. Then the first tear gathered — and like a raindrop hitting a windowpane, it began a slow descent as a rivulet, until more and more followed, and he collapsed onto the floor and curled up, pulling his knees into his chest as tight as he could.

At school the next day, he entered the boys' restroom to pee. Just as he zipped up, several boys shuffled in.

"Hey, Billy!" one of them said. "I heard you like dick."

Billy froze. David must have said something. He closed his eyes, drew in a breath, and turned around. He recognized the three boys — all them on the baseball team.

He tilted his head. "Dick who? Van Dyke?"

The boys stared at him.

"Oh," he said, "that one went over your heads. I'll aim lower next time." He took a step to leave, but one of the boys blocked his path.

"Not so fast," the first boy said. "You need to learn what happens to homos like you."

He nodded to the boy blocking Billy. He quickly moved around behind him, slipped his arms under Billy's, and pulled him back to hold him. Billy squirmed, but the boy's grip was vicelike, and if Billy had tried any harder to pull away, the boy would probably have popped his shoulder sockets.

The first boy took a swing, driving his fist into Billy's belly. Before Billy could cry out from the shock and pain, the boy slammed another fist into his cheek, just below his left eye.

"Please!" Billy screamed. "Stop!"

The boy punched him once more in the face. Billy went limp, his mind a haze of images and thoughts, his body aching, his face a patchwork of pain, throbbing, throbbing, throbbing. The boy holding him released his grip and dropped him to the floor, kicked him in the side, and the three exited laughing.

"Fucking faggot," one of them muttered.

When Billy was finally able, he lifted himself from the tiled bathroom floor, steadied himself against the sink, and looked in the mirror. Welts and bruises had already formed. He turned on the cold water, splashed some on his face, drank some from cupped hands, splashed his face some more, and then dabbed with a paper towel to dry off. He reached down and lifted his shirt. Another large bruise had already formed where he'd been kicked. He touched it and flinched. Maybe he'd fractured a rib. He trudged over to the wall by the door and waited, listening for the bell to ring. When he finally heard the signal that everyone should be back in class, he picked up his backpack and left. The hallway was empty, quiet. With ginger steps, he emerged, then slunk down the corridor and headed for the front entrance. No way was he going to the principal's office. Pushing back tears, he stumbled home and crawled into bed.

That evening, his stepfather looked up from the TV when Billy emerged from his room for dinner. His lips drew back into a smile. "I figured this would happen." Then he went back to watching the early evening news.

His mother ignored the comment, chastised Billy for getting into fights, and then went about setting the table. Billy slumped into a family room chair, thought about David, and wondered if he'd deserved what he'd gotten. Fate had marked him — a loner, an emotional hermit, a pansy.

It was a long while before he approached another guy.

❈

He mentally checks where he is in the set. He only has to be funny for another twenty minutes or so. Then he can retreat to the dressing room, have a shot of vodka, and close his eyes.

"So I was in Lowe's the other day, and I was looking at paint samples. You ever notice the names they give paint colors? Like Mushroom Bisque."

Some chuckles. He gestures with his hand, swiping it across the space in front of him, as though reading a marquee.

"Charismatic Sky."

More chuckles.

"Secret Meadow."

Chuckles begin to subside.

"You know that some gay guy is making up those paint names. If straight men labeled those cans they'd be brown, blue, and green."

Laughter, especially from the women. Someone in the front row is nodding her head.

"See? She knows. Am I right?" He starts to walk around the stage. "I remember when I first wore this jacket, I asked my straight friend, Mark, if he liked it. He said, 'Yeah, you look good in brown.'"

He stops in his tracks on the stage, his face contorted.

"Brown? BROWN?"

Laughter begins to bubble.

"Mark, honey, this is not brown!" He stands tall and with a flourish of his hand, says, "This is Ravishing Cocoa."

Widespread laughter.

"Ravishing Cocoa. I had just broken up with someone and was a bit down when I went to work for a paint company. No, this is a true story. I figured I could make up paint names. After two weeks, the boss called me in and said there was a problem. He said my paint names were hostile. I said, 'Hostile? What's wrong with Bitter Bitch Beige?'"

Laughter.

"'Eat Me Eggplant.'"

Laughter. He raises his voice and almost shouts the last name.

"'Fuck You Fuchsia.'"

There is a combination of applause and laughter. He paces as he waits for the reaction to die down. His mind starts to wander. Internally, he tells himself to snap back, remember where he is, what he's doing. The applause begins to fade.

✻

In college, Billy discovered that some married men liked to have sex on the side with other men. He was a student at Cal State Sacramento, majoring in English and Communication, not sure where a degree would lead him, but reading had always been his escape — and understanding the power of language seemed important to him.

During the fall of his junior year, Professor Young stopped him after class.

"You have a moment, Billy?"

"Sure."

Young was in his forties, medium build, and decent looking Billy thought, but nothing like the type he was most attracted to. He knew as an adult he was still looking for a David, for that baseball player from middle school grown up, for that straw-colored hair and eyes that rivaled a jeweller's array of sapphires. Young was none of that, yet Billy was mildly curious as to why the professor wanted to speak to him.

"I was wondering if you'd like to grab a coffee sometime. I'd like to talk to you about your future."

"You read palms on the side?"

His teacher chuckled. "No. I mean your plans."

Billy shrugged.

"How about now?" Young asked.

Billy had no more classes for the day and a coffee sounded like a good idea. Again, curiosity nibbled around the edges of his thoughts. "Okay. Sure."

Within a week, Young had arranged for them to meet at a hotel, and Billy slid into a routine of after-class trysts with the professor. He knew the man was married, but Billy felt little remorse. Some men married out of shame, pressure, religion or some kind of duty. It was 1980 and although guys his age were increasingly open about their sexuality, the generation that preceded him was not. There was a hole in Billy — he knew it — and something was better than nothing. There were worse things than being the other woman.

Young would check in alone, and Billy would arrive at the appointed time wearing sunglasses and a ballcap, pass through the lobby unnoticed and head up to the room. On one afternoon, just after Billy had left the hotel room, he passed a woman on his way to the elevator. She was agitated and mumbled to herself.

"That cheating son-of-a-bitch."

Billy furrowed his brow while his gaze followed her hurried walk. Within seconds, she was knocking on the door to Young's room. *Holy shit*, he thought. Was that his wife? How'd she know her husband was there? Billy slipped into the elevator and pressed the button. When the doors opened onto the lobby, he rushed to the front entrance and dashed to his car. He took in several deep breaths, started the engine, and pulled away. He shook his head. *What was I thinking? Sooner or later married men get caught, don't they?* He thanked the stars the woman had not seen him come out of the room and that no one knew who he was or that he'd been there.

That evening the eleven o'clock news led with a story about a local professor. Sitting in his apartment with his roommate, Billy leaned in as an image of Young appeared next to the newscaster.

"A professor at Cal State here in Sacramento was shot by his wife earlier today, who then took her own life. The incident transpired in the Double Tree . . ."

Billy's jaw went slack.

"Hey, that's Professor Young," his roommate said. "Don't you have a class with him?"

Billy nodded absentmindedly, his gaze fixed on the screen, his stomach roiling with emotions that threatened to erupt into a spew of vomit.

"The motive is not clear for this murder-suicide and anyone with information may contact the authorities at . . ."

Billy closed his eyes.

"Wow," his roommate muttered.

In his room later, Billy retraced all his steps over the previous two months, his mind sorting out a jumble of questions about who might have seen him, who might have known, whether the police would show up knocking on his door. But he hadn't really been involved. The crime had happened after he left. His hands were clean, weren't they? Still . . .

Weeks dragged on — Billy constantly working to keep his nerves in check, not to let on to his roommate, not to let anyone know how he'd become a professor's piece of ass on the side. Off and on he also contemplated how close he himself had come to death. What would have happened if

Young's wife had arrived minutes before? Bam! A bullet into Billy, too. Shit.

A new instructor took over Young's class, and eventually, the hubbub over the professor's death gave way to the shock of John Lennon's murder on the streets of New York. Billy's confidence grew that he would never be linked to Young in any way — and by the time finals were over, he was anxious for a break. That was when he realized he never mourned the death of his professor. Somehow, he'd never felt the need.

When he returned from Christmas break, he spied a flyer. Large block letters announced an extra-curricular eight-week class. MAKE 'EM DIE LAUGHING. Billy mulled over the thought. He was going to turn twenty-one, and he had difficulty imagining a future. The past clung to him like an invisible cloak, not letting him see beyond the next day, the next week. Images of his childhood, his teenage years, his life now — they never seemed to go away. He needed something different, an escape, a new focus. He joined the class and on day one, the instructor asked him, "Are you funny?"

"Only if you look at me naked," he deadpanned.

The group laughed. He'd found his hammer.

*

Time to wrap up. He has done his job. The next day the *Mercury News* would say he gave another rave performance.

"Ladies, here's the test to see if a man is gay. You sing a line from any song from a musical, but you leave off the end. If he can complete it, he's gay!"

Laughter.

"No. It works. It really works. Ladies, don't participate. Watch this." He starts to sing. "Clang, clang went the . . ."

He holds out his microphone toward the audience. Shouts of male voices singing "trolley" fill the auditorium. Laughter erupts.

"My god! This crowd is like last call at the ManHole."

More laughter. He points to a woman in the front row.

"Oh my, look at her. She's jabbing her husband with her elbow. 'How do you know that? I'll be talking to you when we get home!'"

More laughter. He looks out at the entire crowd.

"And if that test doesn't work, just ask him what color this is." He tugs at the bottom of his jacket. "If he says 'brown', drop your dress, flash your tits, and have at him."

Some laughs.

"But if he says 'Ravishing Cocoa'..." He lowers his voice, almost to a whisper, "...check the closet for size twelve high-heels."

Laughter. He raises his hand high.

"Goodnight, everyone! Thank you!"

People jump to their feet, the resounding applause almost drowning out his exit music.

"Thank you so much!" He shouts this into his mic. "San Jose, you're great!"

He bows, throws a kiss, and walks off. The stage manager pats him on the back.

"Good show," he says.

"Thanks."

He high-fives several others working sound and lights, then saunters to his dressing room. Inside, he plops onto his chair, reaches for his bag, and pulls out a flask. He tugs on the vodka, lets his head roll back as he looks at the ceiling. He feels the adrenaline slowing in his body, the stage-high wearing off. He inhales deeply, then reaches into his bag for something else and holds it up to read. It's an obituary for David Allman, sent to him the day before by a private detective he'd hired. It's dated October 12, 2000, ten years ago, and says that David died of AIDS-related complications in San Francisco. He was survived by his siblings, his mother, and his partner-in-life, Stuart Jensen.

"I always knew," he says.

He sets the piece of paper down, takes another swig of vodka, and looks in the mirror. He touches his lips, a flood of images pushing at his consciousness, a post-show dam cracked open so that memories as far back as four-years-old rush forward to drown out the present. After a moment, the flood recedes. He's back in his dressing room, still gazing into the mirror. He draws his mouth into a small grin and harumphs.

"Kiss my pansy ass," he says.

Bill VanPatten

Complete and Utter Loss

December 1973 was deadly at our house. We had the tree, a balsam pine bought at the lot behind the closed Tas-T-Freeze. The crèche was out, even the lamb without a head, and there were presents. Stevie gave me a Bonnie Bell sampler set and I gave him one for Canoe. I guess we know who shopped at Walgreen's. Mother bought me a Donkenny outfit from Wiebolt's; Grandma Betty said I could go to Chandler's and pick out some new shoes with the money she gave me. Matt was the hard one this year because he was too old for toys but too young for a lot of other things, so Mom and Dad bought him a stereo and Stevie and I were jealous, but we came around and bought him a few albums. I gave him one of my favorites, Traffic, *The Low Spark of High-Heeled Boys*. I asked him to look at the picture of the band on the cover, but he saw nothing unusual, while my girlfriends and I were sure Jim Capaldi stuffed his pants with socks, the bulge was so huge. Dad gave Mom a necklace, a heart outlined in diamond chips, and she cried. But there was another present, he said, and handed her another tiny box. When she opened it, she burst into tears. "It's the engagement ring I couldn't afford when we got married," he said, "Better late than never."

For a half-second I was sure there was a joke in there somewhere, but the only thing I could think of was something about her 'late husband' and, of course, there was nothing funny about that phrase. My parents and we kids knew, even if we would never have said it, that this was probably Dad's last Christmas. We acted like it was just another happy holiday for the Mehaneys, but it was all pretend. No-one wanted to admit the truth.

The day after Christmas, my Dad started cobalt treatments again. He was taking pills and slept a lot. One night he woke the whole house with screaming. He had a dream about a baby that turned into a pig. We all woke up wired, on alert. It wasn't like we could hear what he was saying in his sleep, but we could hear the distress in his voice, and Mom woke him just as I was peeking my head in the room. "Johnnie, Johnnie, wake up," she told him, and gently shook him. There was my Father, the hair grown sparse and the face thinned out, awake and vulnerable-looking.

"In the closet, next to the shoe trees, there was an abandoned baby, squalling his eyes out," he said with such urgency that both Mother and I looked at him intently, "and when I went to pick it up, it turned into a pig, and the baby was gone." Dad made as if he was going to check out the closet but he couldn't move that fast anymore. He could barely shrug in that general direction. So, I did it. I opened the closet door wide and moved around the things on the floor, "See Dad, there's nothing. Just shoes."

He put his head back on the pillow again and closed his eyes. I looked at Mother who was tentative as she lay back down too, her hand reaching from under the blankets to him.

We all tried to go back to sleep. I heard Matt's and Stevie's beds creak as they rolled over, and Matt yelled out "Dad?" I went to their room and told them quietly that it was all right, they could go back to bed; Dad just had a bad dream. But it was like we all had the bad dream. No-one could get right back to sleep

The next day none of us left the house. My brothers didn't want to go to Horner Park to ice skate on the frozen basketball court, and when the Sewells, our neighbors from down the alley, called to say they were taking their toboggan to Caldwell Woods, neither of the boys wanted to go. We all stuck close to home.

I set up the card table in the living room, near his recliner chair. I started the jigsaw puzzle I gave him for Christmas, "Country Barn", 1,500 pieces, hoping Dad would come out and help. But it wasn't until New Year's Eve that he came out of his room and by then I'd finished it.

Earlier in the fall, when Dad had been sick after his first treatments, he stayed in that chair 12 hours a day, from morning until night, watching TV, yelling every once in a while for me or my brothers to change the channels for him. He joked he was getting saddle sores from sitting in that leather chair so long. When I was down in the basement, doing a load of wash, the sheets from the bed, I found a little straw cowboy hat that used to be Matt's. I brought it up and crowned him with it. "Ride 'em, cowboy," I'd said then, and we all laughed because it looked so ridiculous. The candy-striped cord only went under his nose, not his chin. The hat perched on his head made him look like Ed Wynn.

With the pig dream, all the humor was sucked from the house. There was nothing funny about our waiting. In early February, the news was all about Patty Hearst and her kidnapping. "See," said Grandma Betty, "even the rich have problems."

It was February 22. I was in big trouble with Sister Hartwig because I used *Cliffs Notes* for my paper on *Macbeth*. I knew she was disappointed in me, hurt really. After all, I was one of her favorites; everyone knew it, not just me. On top of everything else, I was kind of belligerent about it, not backing down, not apologetic or grovelling. After all, how could I give a shit about Shakespeare? I tried, but I hated taking time to look over on the footnote page and see what the heck his characters were talking about. And the other thing, the thing I would still argue today, was that the author, whom Sister called "Old Will" like it was a big joke, didn't sit down and write the play thinking "Okay, now I'll put a symbol here and this will represent such and such, so people years from now will interpret it that way." No, he wrote plays he wanted people to see and enjoy. Authors sit down and they just write. They tell a good story, or even a bad one, and it was stupid that people hundreds of years later tried to analyze it so much. Why couldn't we just leave it be? Why ruin literature by analyzing it over and over? It was what Grandma Betty called beating a dead horse. Often during that winter, thinking made me tired.

Besides, on those nights when I should have been reading Shakespeare, I sat up with my Dad. I sat right next to the TV for him and changed the channels when he told me to. Sometimes he'd make me turn and turn. Other times, he'd get occupied by Carson or Cavett or the late movie. It was just me and him. Everyone else was sleeping. The living room was dark except for the TV. If I didn't do this for Dad, he'd be stuck with commercials. He'd be stuck with a Gabor on *The Tonight Show* or somebody boring being interviewed on Dick Cavett. It was something I could do for him, changing the channels.

That was what going through my brain as Sister Hartwig confronted me about my paper, which I wouldn't admit came straight from *Cliffs Notes*. "Sister," I lied, "I did write this on my own. It is my work." Then she got out her own copy of the *Cliffs Notes* and I knew I was fucked. She pointed out phrases I had used. Still I wouldn't fess up. Shakespeare was too hard, I wanted to tell her, but something prevented me from giving an inch. The corner I backed myself into got smaller and tighter. "I didn't copy," I said. That was when she told me to go down to my locker and get my notes. So, I took the long way down there, walking past two girls I knew had been eavesdropping, through the Learning Resource Center, which had recently been remodelled. It was once the chapel but now it was emptied of church things and filled with tables and bookcases. I could still smell the glue from the new carpeting.

I walked back from my locker even more slowly, knowing I would get caught in a lie when Peggy Vaughan walked by, "I heard your name over the PA," she said, "You have a telephone call at the office." I flashed her the bullshit sign; we were always gooning each other like that. She said, "No, really." I went past the office and there was Mrs. Gregg waiting in the doorway. She handed me the receiver and Grandma Betty was on the phone.

"Elizabeth, come home," she said, "your father." That was all I needed to hear to know it was bad. Plus, she told me to take a cab, so I knew it was really bad because I had never taken a cab before. Mrs. Gregg called the taxi and then I went back to the Learning Resource Center to find Sister Hartwig. I was trying not to cry but I could feel my face going red and piggy. When I told her I had to go home, she questioned me. "Sister," I said and water escaped from each eye, "Sister, my father is sick, honest." Then she asked how I was getting home and I told her Mrs. Gregg had called a cab, and Sister said to get my things from my locker and she would meet me at the side door on Rosemont and we could talk some more.

It was raining, a light freezing rain, and we stood there, me and her. She kept looking at me, waiting for me to let loose with the truth, but from the back of my stomach to the back of my head, there was a dam, holding everything in place; I couldn't say a thing. I held my lips closed. I tried not to breathe. I looked for the cab and finally it was there. But before I left, she grabbed my sleeve and looked me in the eyes, "Is your father really sick, Elizabeth."

"Yes, Sister," I said, rushing out, "really."

By the time I got to 4535, Matt and Stevie were already home. Of course, Grandma Betty was there and her friend who we called Aunt Joan, even though she was not related to us, and I could hear that someone was in the kitchen, but before anything else, I ran up the stairs to him.

What had happened to my Father? Mom was beside him on the bed and he seemed so small next to her. I stood at the foot of the bed, half-kneeling, and I said hello. "I took a cab home," I said and it sounded so stupid, so babyish, like it was a big deal to take a cab.

I wish I could say he said something meaningful to me or nodded his head in a special way or that I could tell something special by looking in his eyes, but I can only say this: I didn't want to be there. He wasn't my Dad, the Dad I knew. He was a little old man, crabbed and birdlike and I didn't want to see him die. "That's nice, honey," he said, "Now go get yourself something to eat."

I didn't even tell him I loved him. It was such an obvious thing and yet it didn't occur to me. I wasn't thinking. It was like I shut down. Grandma Betty was there and I had never seen her so sad, crumpled like newspaper. My Mother was glued to my father, holding him, her arms cradling his head. Matt and Stevie were at the foot of the bed now, the shirttails of their uniform shirts hanging out of their pants. Stevie had shoved his navy blue tie in his shirt pocket and now it half dangled out like a tongue. Matt had a Maltese cross inked on his hand. The room was crowded and I didn't know what to do. I fled the scene.

In the hallway, I leaned back on the wall and let myself slide down. My head was almost juxtaposed with his on the other side. I put my head on my knees and covered myself with my hands. Grandma Betty made a noise, almost like the sound a cat makes, which was crazy since she hates cats. My Mother, she said something real quiet and then she started crying. I had never heard her cry like that before, like a little girl. I remembered crying like that once or twice when I was real young, when I cried so hard I could hardly breathe. It was like this for a long time. Quiet except for our Mother's sobs.

All of us were stunned, maybe. It was Grandma Betty who moved first, off to call John Golding at Dunward and Golding Funeral Home, and Dr. Varon, I suppose. I went to my room, lay down on my stomach, doing the dead man's float, thinking that maybe if I just stayed there until it was all over, I could wake up again to a different truth, a regular life.

When I did wake again some of it was over. I mean someone had come and gotten him and Grandma Betty's friends from the Altar & Rosary Society came with food, and the phone was ringing and ringing. Aunt Joan sat at the telephone table in the hall and took the calls — Grandma Betty's sister from New York, Grandma and Grandpa Methy from downstate, and my Mother's brother, Uncle Cal, Uncle Joel, all the cousins.

That night the house was too busy; there was commotion non-stop. Neighbors came by with offers to help once they had seen the hearse outside. That was just how it was where we lived — everybody knew everybody else's business. Normally it was a drag, but that day it was even worse. Their coming over with casseroles or cookies was supposed to console us but it didn't.

I had never seen Grandma Betty like this before. She had shrunk before our eyes. Everything about her was smaller; her eyes were little as raisins, and she wrung her hands constantly, and there was something different about her voice. My brothers seemed younger, not the bold pot-smokers. Matt even put his thumb in his mouth. Stevie was so quiet, sullen almost, like how he was when he got into trouble.

My Mother? I saw her too as I had never seen her before. It was like she was missing something, like she'd come down to the table undressed because something about her was not there, visibly absent, if that makes any sense. She had always been in Dad's presence and now that presence was gone. It was as if the funniest person at the party left, leaving us blank. We were awkward, uncomfortable, all of us drifting.

It was always easiest to talk like that, in comparisons, in metaphors. It was hardest to say what it was really like. Sure, I was adrift. Like I'd been on a big iceberg and a little piece of it broke off, leaving me to float by myself in a big ocean. In reality, Dad's death hit me physically, it came on like the flu. I didn't want to eat or talk or sleep. I just wanted to sit there and have everybody leave me alone. But of course, that couldn't be. Like I said, the phone was ringing non-stop, the doorbell was chiming every so often and I didn't want Mom or Grandma Betty to have to do everything.

Grandma Betty took over dealing with the other grownups, with the arrangements. When Aunt Joan took a break, I tried to answer some of the phone calls. When my friend Jenny called, we spoke for a while, talked about school (she got a demerit in gym class for not having her uniform) and the boys we knew (she'd heard Gill broke it off with Bonnie), and Cary's impending wedding (could we really believe it) and it was about ten minutes into this small talk before I could tell her.

"I got to get off now," I said, "The phone's real busy. My Dad died today."

"Really," said Jenny, incredulous, perhaps first unbelieving at the way I snuck that fact into the conversation and then probably surprised because I never really talked about how sick my Dad was, had avoided the subject in any way, shape, or form. Besides, my Dad was much younger than all the other fathers. "Are you serious, Liz?" she asked a couple of times.

"Yeah," I said and could add nothing more.

"Shit," she said.

"Yeah, no shit," I said, "See you."

I'd had no sooner hung up when the phone rang again. It was Sister Hartwig.

"Elizabeth, I am so sorry," she said, and I wondered how she knew. I guessed that Grandma Betty or Aunt Joan must have made a lot of calls while I was in my room. "I am so sorry I doubted you," she said again because I didn't answer back, didn't say anything, just stared at a spot on the wallpaper as if I was looking across the telephone wires.

"It's okay Sister Hartwig, I never said."

"I should have taken your word for it," she said again, "I am so sorry," she repeated, a strain of urgency or sincerity or something in her voice.

"That's okay," I said.

"Sorry, really, truly," she said.

"My paper," I began but she cut me off.

"It's okay about the paper," she said.

I didn't say anything, didn't know what to say. My father was dead but at least I didn't have to do the Macbeth paper. What luck.

"And," there was another pause, "Elizabeth, you can tell me things, you could have told me your father was sick. If you want to talk to somebody in the future, you can talk to me," she said.

Then she said other things that I didn't remember because I was thinking I couldn't tell her anything. How could you tell a nun you did it? How could she advise you about breaking up with a boy? How do you say someone you love is dying? And the things she wanted to hear, the stuff about how I was searching for myself, that was stuff I couldn't even articulate. All that gooey tripe about finding my identity, finding out what I was really about, that was the stuff grownups wanted to hear. That was the regular teenage stuff they liked to hear because they thought you were confiding in them, that they were your buddies. Then they could tell you something profound like "Be yourself" and feel better about themselves. All that shit about being on the threshold of adulthood, that was what they lived for. The real stuff, they didn't want to know, and I didn't want to share. Not with her. Not with anyone.

Especially then I didn't want to talk to anybody. Nothing in the world interested me. My Father was dead.

Mom was worried because Matt's dress pants were out at the knee and he would need new ones. She said, "You can walk up to Spaulding's tomorrow with him and get him some new ones." I said okay, not correcting, not pointing out we never went to Spaulding's anymore, hadn't shopped there for years, not after she had pronounced Spaulding's merchandise cheapo. Also, I could drive Matt to any store. I couldn't figure out why she said Spaulding's and it wasn't until Grandma Betty heard us talking that she said, "Spaulding's?" Mother looked at her, one of those stares like in a Hitchcock movie where the heroine is all confused, "Did I say Spaulding's? Of course, Elizabeth, you knew what I meant."

"Yeah," I said but I was confused. What had made her hark back to those days? When she asked if I needed something she never waited for my answer but corrected herself, "No, you don't need anything, you have that plaid skirt you got at Christmas." She said, "You do know you have to wear a skirt," and I said I knew that but I said it real nice, not at all smart-alecky or snotty. Did she really expect me to say I wanted to wear my blue jeans? I said maybe I needed a new pair of opaque tights and she said okay.

Spaulding's. It was at the restaurant across from Spaulding's that Dad took Mom for that fried shrimp dinner when he was staying at the Heart o' Chicago. I wondered, stupidly, would she ever look at fried shrimp the same way again? Would I, for that matter.

The next day was weird because nobody woke us up. We got to sleep until practically the afternoon and when we did wake up the house was real quiet. Quiet as a tomb. Then I started to cry.

Ellen Wade Beals

Ours is the trying

Walking from the train, Hetty kept reliving the conversation with the printer. After months of frustration, it was all 'yes'.

"Yes, I can get hold of handmade paper."

"Really? And the vegetable inks?"

"Yes. And no problem with the illustrations."

Her next book of poems was, finally, going to be all sustainable.

She'd parked outside one of the new houses near the station turn-off. Saved the extortionate parking charge in the skimpy station car park. Why did they build stations so far outside villages? She could have done the whole trip more quickly by car but you had to do your bit for the planet. The triumph at finding a green craft printer meant she could have eased up on herself a bit. But you can't fool yourself like that can you? There was a message scrawled on a piece of paper under her windscreen wiper.

'Do NOT park outside my house. This is NOT the station car park.'

She screwed it up. She'd had worse but it was still aggression and it still hurt. She stood for a few minutes to breathe deeply as some members of the Hunt, out on exercise, rode by with the pack tailing. Hetty breathed even more deeply, reeling at the reek of superiority that came from the red-coated riders. Those poor noble horses. Those poor faithful dogs. She thought of the old soldiers, the redcoats and their male power that came from wearing the colour of blood.

It was a quarter-hour drive to the village on the winding road through the Wealden woods. The tarmac was dappled with June midday sunlight breaking through the trees overhead. She remembered her mother's saying: 'Where the tree tops meet there are fairies.' Her phone rang in its dashboard cradle.

"Sal!" Sally ran the artist's collective gallery in Lewes.

"Hiya — good news. You won't believe it. We've sold five of your watercolours this week — framed. They love the ones of your garden. Have you got any more — and can you bring some poems?"

"Sal, that's fantastic! Sorry darling — I'm driving. Call you back soon."

From good to better. She'd have to get a proper horoscope done. She caught sight of her face in the side mirror. Long grey hair spilling out of her headscarf. Bright grey eyes laughing above lined cheeks. Isn't it great being old! Everything working out.

Just before her cottage, the last at the edge of the village, she slowed in case there were any deer crossing. Not today. She indicated and turned into one of her own watercolours. Ox-eye daisies clamoured on the uncut verge. They were enormous, egg yolk yellow against perfect white. She'd not cut the lawn at all this year either, and there were cornflower blues and red poppies all come from nowhere. The little weatherboarded cottage itself seemed to grow out of the foliage. A red admiral fluttered past her and she imagined the hidden world of beetles, worms, spiders, grubs in all that beautiful chaos. So wonderful to be part of the whole intricate world of living things. Trees talking to each other through their roots, birds navigating by magnetism. 'What's it like to be a spider,' she thought, 'down there?'

There were two envelopes on the mat. She recognised the writing on the first — Michael — and smiled. The other envelope was blank. Her shoulders tightened, she sensed it was one of those, and left it there. She went and got her silver letter opener and gently prised open Michael's envelope. He'd made the card himself. A cartoon daisy and the single word 'Peace'. Inside he'd written 'All the best on your 70th birthday'. How sweet of him. Michael, her ally in the uncut verge campaign, lived further down in the village. He went all the way back to art school. Now, bless him, he didn't know what to do with the stray hairs that grew on his bald top. She put the card on the mantelpiece and stood back to admire it.

She returned for the second envelope. Ripped it open with her fingers. It was torn from a notebook, scribbled in thick black felt pen.

'Why aren't you DEAD yet you WOKE COMMUNIST BITCH.'

She held it at the edge between finger and thumb, arm extended. She fumbled at the front door latch with her other hand, pulled it open stumbled along the uneven path around the side of the cottage and finally flung the card on the compost heap. She remembered to breathe deeply.

Four in,

hold for four,

four out.

She was walking back round to her front door, shaking, as the Asp next door came out to inspect his BMW convertible, parked by the much larger Mercedes. He carried an open toolbox full of polishes and cloths. There was an antiseptic lawn by the extensive tarmac drive with narrow borders of roses and peonies. She'd given up even saying 'good morning'. There was no point, he would simply ignore her. Plenty of people thought they had cause to hate her. She'd petitioned against the hunt, opposed the new houses, written to the local paper about how it was essential not to cut verges. Some villagers looked edgy when she said 'good morning.' Others ignored her completely. She went back in and made herself an infusion, wishing Michael could still walk round to see her. But his uncut lawn, which had once been a conscious decision, was now a necessity as his legs deteriorated. She might drop by on her way to Lewes.

It was Michael who had thought of calling Next Door 'the Asp'. Short for aspirational. They'd all come over the past few years as a local builder infilled every empty space in the village. His final work, just before his fatal heart attack, had been the house next door. He'd loved tarmac, and the people who'd moved in did too. Hetty thought of all those poor lives crushed beneath it. She and Michael had objected to planning permission. But the house was built and they realised they'd lost. So they resorted to satire behind closed doors. They had a double act at the poetry group.

Hetty: 'On a Sunday morning those lawns start to growl.'

Michael: 'Back off you bastards. I'm having a military haircut.'

Hetty: 'Platoons of peonies sway well-fed in the border tilth.'

Michael: 'Regiments of roses sharpen their thorns.'

Both Together: 'We'll be best in show. We'll rule the world again. We'll take back control of nature!'

A serious poem had come of it for her collection. She recited to herself:

'... *beetles, spiders, things too small for names*
shredded and spit out
the mower moves in perfect lines,
a raster scan as regular as
Sunday lunch...'

She made herself a falafel and salad sandwich. Her address and her car number had been trolled. Her innocent letter about insects had brought furious responses. 'Uncut lawns attract vermin. How can our children play safely? Have these people no self-respect? Lowering the tone of the village. The council should cut it for them and send them the bill.'

There was loud bang in the road, followed by a terrifying groan. She rushed out. There was a deer staggering in the road. There was a car. The car was reversing away from the deer it had hit. It stopped. It was driving forward around the deer. It was accelerating.

"Hey!" She screamed. "Come back! Bastard!" The car accelerated faster.

The deer was bellowing terribly. It struggled to the roadside and collapsed onto the Asp's verge. She could see it was hopeless, the absurd angle of the back legs, the back bent impossibly. Its chest rising and falling, groans coming more frequently.

She found herself kneeling down, by its head. It was beyond trying to escape. She reached out to stroke the top of its head, between the ears. "Ssshhhh," she soothed. The chestnut hide was warm and soft, shiny with summer health, not coarse and dry like she'd imagined.

The Asp was running down his drive. "Has someone been hit?" He saw Hettie and the deer. "Bloody things. Nuisance. They should all be shot. For God's sake don't touch it. It's got disease. You'll infect us all."

"Ssshhhh." She said to the deer, to herself, to the Asp.

"You're an old mad woman. You should be locked up. I've seen the rubbish you write to the papers. I'm calling the police. They can deal with it."

"Ssshhhh." The groans and the breathing continued. She settled into a rhythm with the stroking. She thought of the seasons. The flow of life and death. The beauty, the transience of it all. She was part of something that the deer was part of. It would die she knew. That was inevitable. But she would be there.

The Asp was on his phone, pacing his drive. "They're coming," he called. "I'd leave it alone." He shook his head and went back up his drive.

What could the police do? She knew they would be too late. There was just her and death. A faint smell of musk and wet dog rose from the deer's hide. To her it smelt sweet. She lay down beside it, began to talk gently, soft words just coming from nowhere, like the wildflowers on her lawn. The sudden movements of its eyes settled and she saw iridescent orange in them. Time would not matter, she would just stay here.

A noisy engine and a rattling trailer. It was a dingy green Land Rover. Farmer probably. He had a thin face, thirty maybe, below his flat cap. He assessed the situation and carefully parked on the other side of the Asp's house. He came over. A Barbour and waterproof trousers. He looked the deer over. Saw the skewed legs and the twisted back.

"Poor thing," he said, "she's in a bad way. Have you called the hunt?"

Hetty raised herself to a kneel, still stroking. Her throat tightened. "I do not support the hunt," she said slowly, "that idiot in there called the police."

He nodded. "You've got your views," he said. "Police won't do much. Hunt's the best thing. She'll just die here in pain, rot away. I've got a trailer. I can take her. We can't just leave her here."

It was the 'she' that did it. Whatever his views, he understood. He understood. The dogs would eat the meat. Nothing wasted. Red in tooth and claw. But the cycle. Inevitable.

"Won't be a minute."

He came back with a small cloth bag. And pulled out a hunting knife in a leather sheath.

"Let's put her out of her misery," he said gently.

The tears welled into Hetty's eyes and overflowed. Again it was the 'her'. 'It' wouldn't have worked. "All right," she said, her mouth hardly moving. "I'll do it. Give me the knife."

"Have you... before?"

"Doesn't matter. Give me the knife."

"Are you sure?" He stared into her face. When he had seen what he needed he gripped the knife's sheath and slowly offered her the handle. He understood. The darling little man understood and didn't try to talk her out of it.

He found the vessel with his fingertips and showed her where to slice. "Hard," he said, "and deep. One cut."

The blood flowed. Over the verge, into the road. The groaning stopped.

A police car drew up and the Farmer explained. The Asp arrived. The tentative smooth-faced policeman looked relieved. "Thank you sir, we'd have done just the same. We'll help you get it on your trailer. Give us a hand sir?" he asked the Asp.

"I'm not touching that."

The farmer and the policemen got the carcass on to the trailer.

"We'll be off."

"Aren't you going to clear this up?"

"Not our Job sir."

"I demand somebody clears up this mess. I'm phoning the Council."

Something dark flitted through the Farmer's face. "Try water, sir. You can get it from taps."

Two weeks later, all traces of the blood were gone. The proof copy of her book had arrived.

'... *beetles, spiders, things too small for names*
shredded and spit out

the mower moves in perfect lines,
a raster scan as regular as
Sunday lunch…

….The anonymous notes
The letters to the press
The trolling of the website
….. Tired of these voices
I wonder
why so many lifetimes
have been sacrificed
for a few metres of aspirational desert.'

A small victory. Just one tiny thing — a few pints of oil saved. When out there they were tarmacking over grass, building over farmland, cutting down whole forests. She went out to admire the ox-eyes, now starting to droop, and saw her next-door neighbour at it again, polishing his BMW. 'He's terrified,' she thought suddenly. 'He's terrified that someone will move the goalposts and he won't know what to do.'

"Lovely morning," she said. And he made a faint smile.

Keith Willson

About the Authors

David W. Berner is the author of several award-winning books of fiction and memoir. He has been honoured as the Writer-in-Residence at the Jack Kerouac Project in Florida, and the Ernest Hemingway Birthplace Home and Museum in Oak Park, Illinois. His short stories and poems have been published in literary journals and online editions.

Susan M. Breall is the 2022 winner of the Gateway Review flash fiction contest. Her short stories appear in numerous anthologies including *Impermanent Facts*, *Running Wild Press*, *Kairos Literary Magazine*, *The Raw Art Review*, *Aba Terra anthology*, *Beyond Queer Words*, *Dreamers Creative Writing*, *The Good Life Review*, and Paragon Press' *Martian Chronicle*. By day she handles cases involving abuse, abandonment and neglect of children. By night she writes fiction.

Allison Collins is editor of Upstate Life Magazine and a writer with *The Daily Star* and *Kaatskill Life Magazine*. Her work has been published in online and print journals. Allison lives in upstate New York with her family.

Russell Doherty has studied with George Saunders, Greg Iles, and Joshua Mohr, and attended the Writer's Digest, Santa Barbara, and Kauai Writers Conferences. Russ has a double BA from UCSB in Screenwriting and Music Composition. His work is published in *Ellipsis*, *Evening Street Review*, *Glint Literary Journal*, *Havik*, *Lunaris Review*, *The Opiate*, *The Quiet Reader*, and *Summerset Review*. His short story "The Towers" is published in *Potato Soup Journal's Best of 2021* anthology. Russ walks the beach a lot, arguing with the characters in his head. He also loves to travel with his family.

Stephen Elmer lives and works in Ventura County, California, where he builds software by day and creates stories by night (and early, early morning). His stories mix quirky, satirical characters with social commentary on a wide variety of topics. When he isn't reading, he can be found playing games with his two sons or biking around town looking for great food.

Siobhan Gifford lives and writes in an old cottage in the shadow of the North York Moors which historically housed the village witch. A former journalist, her work has appeared in newspapers, magazines and various anthologies; in 2023, three poems were chosen for the Ripon Poetry Festival anthology *Creative Juices*, one appeared in *New Contexts: 5* and a fifth poem was Highly Commended in the King Lear Prizes. Siobhan loves playing with the mosaic of words, fitting them together to weave a story or pattern a poem. She is also a mosaic artist.

Susan Perkins lives in North Yorkshire and writes mainly short poems and stories.

Jenna Plewes has 2 pamphlets and 7 collections in print. *The Salt and Sweet of Memory*, (Dempsey and Windle, December 2019), *The Underside of Things* (Hedgehog Poetry Press, 2020), *A Woven Rope* (V. Press, 2021) and *A Lick of Loose Threads* (Hedgehog Poetry Press, 2021. *The Underside of Things* has raised £1,280 for Childline and the Samaritans, *The Salt and Sweet of Memory* and *A Woven Rope* are both being sold in aid of Freedom from Torture and *A lick of Loose Threads* is raising funds for Doctors Without Borders. She and her husband live in Worcestershire with their collie. She has two children and 4 grandchildren.

David Punter is a writer of stories and poetry. He has lived and worked in many places across the world, including England, Scotland, China and Hong Kong, and is now located in a village near Bristol. His most recent published work includes three poetry collections, *Those Other Fields* (Palewell, 2020), *Stranger* (Cinnamon, 2021) and *Ship's Log* (Bristol Books, 2022), all available from his website, davidpunter.org.

Greta Ross was born in Australia. A retired doctor, she is an active poet and member of SaveAs Writers, Canterbury. Greta graduated MA (Distinction) in Poetry Writing through Newcastle University in 2022. Her poems have appeared in over 30 poetry anthologies and journals, as well as gaining prizes in competitions. She was Canterbury International Poet of the Year 2022. Greta enjoys writing in different styles. Many poems are a response to social and political impacts on society or the natural world. Some of her more unusual poems explore the "underbelly" of human experience with the aim of unsettling readers' expectations.

Debra Tillar has been an archaeologist, a teacher, and a freelance travel and food writer. Her short stories have recently been included in several science fiction anthologies and literary journals. Debra spends most of her time writing, creating art from natural and found objects, and traveling the world (she has visited all seven continents). She grew up in New York City but now lives on the Seacoast of New Hampshire and is currently working on her multi-volume science fiction series, *The Nomad*.

Bill VanPatten is an award-winning author of novels and short stories. Because of his background, gay and Latino characters tend to populate his stories. He left a successful career in academia to return to his native California and write full time. On occasion, he still performs standup comedy. You can find out more at www.billvanpatten.net.

Ellen Wade Beals trained as a journalist, and writes poetry and prose. Her work has appeared in literary magazines, in anthologies and on the web in the US, Ireland, and the UK. Her poem "Between the sheets" appears in the textbook *Everything's a Text* (Pearson 2010). She is editor and publisher of the award-winning anthology *Solace in So Many Words* (2011). "Complete and utter loss" is an excerpt from *The Good and Bad of It*, her yet to be published novel.

Keith Willson is a retired clinical scientist who lives in East Sussex. In 2023 he completed an MA in creative writing at the Open University. His writing has been published in *London Magazine, Hot Tin Roof*, and *New Contexts: 5*. As a labour of love, he is currently completing a biography of the novelist, short story, and travel writer William Sansom.